Murc

Country Cot

Addison Moore

and

Bellamy Bloom

Edited by Paige Maroney Smith

Cover by Lou Harper, Cover Affairs

Published by Hollis Thatcher Press, LTD.

Books by the Authors

Cozy Mysteries

Country Cottage Mysteries
Kittyzen's Arrest (Country Cottage Mysteries 1)
Dog Days of Murder (Country Cottage Mysteries 2)
Santa Claws Calamity (Country Cottage Mysteries 3)
Bow Wow Big House (Country Cottage Mysteries 4)
Murder Bites (Country Cottage Mysteries 5)
Felines and Fatalities (Country Cottage Mysteries 6)

Murder in the Mix
Cutie Pies and Deadly Lies (Murder in the Mix 1)
Bobbing for Bodies (Murder in the Mix 2)
Pumpkin Spice Sacrifice (Murder in the Mix 3)
Gingerbread and Deadly Dread (Murder in the Mix 4)
Seven-Layer Slayer (Murder in the Mix 5)
Red Velvet Vengeance (Murder in the Mix 6)
Bloodbaths and Banana Cake (Murder in the Mix 7)
New York Cheesecake Chaos (Murder in the Mix 8)
Lethal Lemon Bars (Murder in the Mix 9)
Macaron Massacre (Murder in the Mix 10)

My name is Bizzy Baker and I read minds. Not every mind, not every time, but it happens, and believe me when I say, it's not all it's cracked up to be. Like now for instance.

Great news—Georgie Conner leans over the marble counter of the reception area in the Country Cottage Inn—*I found the perfect vacation spot up north. They serve three hot meals a day, have a sundeck available every afternoon, and a library with the complete works of Shakespeare. They have a craft center and yoga classes. It's lights on at five in the morning and lights out at nine. I think I can really dig a place like that.*

I make a face over at the wiry-haired woman before me whom I've grown to love like a grandmother. She's donned a red sequin kaftan in honor of tonight's heart-shaped festivities and she has that twinkle in her blue eyes that tells me she's already having a good time. Georgie is an older woman who I couldn't love more if she was family, and in a way she's just that. My father has married more women over the years than I care to count, and Georgie was once officially his mother-in-law. But unlike the many ex-mothers-in-law my father has amassed that have drifted away, Georgie stayed put, and I'm glad about it, too.

Georgie is one of the very few people who knows I have the ability to read minds, and she does love to put me to the test every now and again—like now for example.

"Georgie, that place you just described sounds either like a psychiatric ward or a prison. I suggest you stay out of both."

She waves me off. "It's a place called Collinsworth."

"Oh my God." I nearly drop the pen right out of my hand. "Georgie, Collinsworth is a women's correctional facility right here in northern Maine. It *is* a prison."

"A *what*?" She inches back. "Well, what's my precious Juniper Moonbeam doing there?"

"What's a Juniper Moonbeam?"

"My daughter. The one that was momentarily detained by way of matrimony to your wedding-hungry father."

"Oh, that's right. *Juni.*" I like to tease that I got Georgie in the divorce. And honest to God, I almost always forget about Juni being the very reason why I got her.

Georgie glowers at the ballroom a moment. "I'll see you at the dance, Biz."

It's not quite a dance we're hosting here tonight at the Country Cottage Inn. I'm not entirely sure what tonight's Cupid-centered chaos could be classified as. But I do know that I can lay the blame squarely on Georgie Conner's colorful shoulders. Georgie met some online love match guru last month who owns and operates a dating app called Dependable. His name is Elvis Hendrix and he's about as artificial and yet colorful as his made-up moniker suggests. Anyway, he asked if he could have the ballroom for a dating event this evening and it seemed harmless enough, so I guess at the end of the day the blame falls squarely on my shoulders instead. Hopefully, some good will come of it and all of the singles in Cider Cove will succumb to Cupid's arrows. We could use a little more lovin' and a lot less murder around these parts. Lord knows we've had our fair share of homicides as of late.

Georgie takes off in a fury just as Deputy Leo Granger strides into the reception area looking dapper with a pair of jeans and a sports coat on top. Leo is a tall, dark-haired man with a wily smile and a devious gleam in his eyes. He's the only other person on the planet that I've openly admitted my mindreading quirk to, but only because he can do it, too. And by his side stands Mayor Mackenzie Woods, my one time best friend who thought it was a good idea to try to drown me while we were in middle school, thus landing me in this mind reading predicament to begin with.

Hello, Bizzy. Leo smiles my way as they pass me. *I hope you'll join the fun. Just because you're dating Jasper doesn't mean you can't have a good time.*

Very funny. I make a face at him. Leo and Jasper used to be best friends once upon a time until Leo thought it was a good idea to steal Jasper's fiancée away from him. They've been on the outs ever since.

I nod over to both Leo and Mackenzie as they proceed to the singles mingle event taking place in the ballroom. Technically, Leo and Mack are already an established couple. I'm betting they're here because Mackenzie feels the need to say a few words. Cider Cove has endured a long line of mayors with the surname Woods, stemming all the way back to her great-grandfather.

Let's be honest. Nostalgia secured her the position when she ran for office, and her own incessant need for attention was the driving force that led her to run in the first place.

Mack is no mayoral angel. Not only did she try to kill me when we were kids, but she proceeded to steal every boyfriend I had in high school. Thankfully, my latest and greatest boyfriend is virtually swipe-proof. I just so happen to be dating the hottest homicide detective in all of Maine, maybe the country, so I'm not single by a long shot. But since I happen to run the Country Cottage Inn, I'll be heading into the ballroom to see what the singles mingle shenanigans are all about.

I sigh dreamily just thinking about Jasper—*Detective* Jasper Wilder. Tall, dark hair, icy gray eyes that demand the attention of every woman in a ten-mile radius, a body built for a SEAL team, and a dangerous smile that you need to work to extract from him. Jasper doesn't know that I have the uncanny ability to pry into his mind, but he does know I have a deep secret I've been keeping from him. And just about a week ago, I let him know that it was time I shared my secret. And as soon as the moon, the sun, the planets, and the stars line up—and maybe a few shots of something strong that will burn its way down my esophagus—I'll do just that. Here's hoping I don't chicken out.

I won't, but believe me I want to.

Jasper is out at the moment helping his mother assess her condo. His mother's place flooded a few months back and she's been staying right here at the inn while her home gets an overhaul. His mother, Gwyneth, and I had a rocky start to our relationship, but it's been a bit better as of late.

She was actually going to marry my father on Christmas Eve, after an all too brief whirlwind—*romance* would be too strong of a word—more like a casual hello, but cooler heads prevailed and they're going to try out this thing called an engagement. I'll admit, the thought of my father engaged to my boyfriend's mother is just plain weird.

A woman bustles through the crowd as she edges her way to the reception counter. Her pale hair is slightly frazzled. Her complexion is pale, too, for the most part, but she has a pop of bright pink lipstick that breathes some life into her face.

She gives a sideways glance toward the ballroom where a majority of the well-dressed crowd is funneling its way into. ***I'd bet good money I was the only one here tonight in an effort to please my mother.***

The wary blonde adjusts her dark blazer. She has a button-down blouse underneath that rises to her neck, and she seems dressed more for a business meeting than she is a night of flirtatious fun. She looks a touch older than me. Early thirties, I'm guessing.

"Hello, welcome to the Country Cottage Inn," I trill in the same sing-songy voice I've used for the last half hour straight to greet the masses. "Are you here for the singles event?" I point toward the ballroom where a large banner reads *Welcome to the Blind Date with Cupid Singles Mingle!*

I bet it *was* her mother who told her all about it and then forced her to come. I was single for a good long while and my own mother tried her best to find me a perfect match. Lucky for me, I happened to stumble upon one last fall, right after I stumbled upon a dead body.

My fingers ride to my lips as if I had spoken the words out loud. That's not exactly what I was trying to say. It may have happened in that order, but I'd like to think Jasper and I would have landed in one another's arms whether or not there was a corpse to bring us together.

The blonde in front of me sheds a tight smile. "Yes, I am here for the event." She leans in. There's a hint of anger in her coffee-colored eyes, but she has an open face and lips that easily glide in the right direction. She seems nice enough. "You wouldn't happen to know if Lad Warner has arrived yet, do you? He's one of the developers of Dependable." She makes a face. "It's the dating app that's sponsoring the event. Their slogan is *romance on demand.*"

"Lad?" I shake my head, unaware of any other developer for that dating app that's responsible for tonight's couples' catastrophe in the making. "Do you mean Elvis? Elvis Hendrix?" I still can't get past his dicey pseudonym. This is his party tonight and the guests are all people who subscribe to his dating app, Dependable.

She shakes her head. "Lad is his partner in Cupid crime. I'm sure I'll find him soon enough." She glares over at the ballroom. *And when I do, I just might kill him.*

A bemused smile quivers on my lips.

She takes off with the rest of the crowd streaming toward the ballroom, and a part of me wonders how worried I should be. It's not like Cider Cove hasn't had its fair share of homicides in the last few months. But then again, saying you're going to kill someone is nothing more than a well-worn euphemism these days.

I take a look around at the interior of the inn. Valentine's Day is just a couple of weeks away and we've gone all out with the pink and red metallic hearts pasted up in every free space. The inn itself has a dark wooden interior that gives it a cozy feel, and every time I set foot inside, it feels as if the inn itself were giving me a hug. The floors are a distressed shade of gray, and there's a grand wrought iron stairwell that leads to the second story. The doors and wainscoting of the expansive foyer are a rich, dark wood heavily inlaid with carvings. The ballroom to my right has seen just about every celebration you can imagine, and there's even a formal dining room for the guests of the facility. The Cottage Café that sits on the back end of the building leads right to the sandy shores of Cider Cove and is open to guests and the public as well. And just like the inn itself, all animals are welcome there, too.

The entry to the inn is framed with pink twinkle lights and an oversized tulle wreathe dotted with pink and red hearts sits over each door. I love how frilly the world gets as we collectively lose our minds in the name of love this time of year. And lucky for me, it's my first year in a long time that I actually get to celebrate it with a love of my own.

"Bizzy?" Nessa Crosby strides up from the ballroom. "You should check out that shindig. And then after you're done checking it out, I want to check it out again. Unlike you, I'm still single, you know." She snips out that last part as if it were entirely my fault.

Nessa is a pretty brunette with lashes longer than should ever be legal, a pert little nose, and perfect bowtie lips. I've known Nessa all my life. I went to school with both her sister and her cousin, Emmie—the latter of which is officially my BFF.

Grady pops up behind her. "Why don't you both head on over? I've seen about all I need."

Grady Pennington is a dark-haired, blue-eyed Irish heartbreaker. Both he and Nessa have been working at the inn ever since they graduated from college a while back. They keep insisting this is just a stepping-stone on the way to their real careers, but if they ever leave the inn I'll be lost without them. They're not only handy to have around, but after all the blood, sweat, and tears we've been through—

and with the killings that have taken place here—they've become like family.

"By the way"— Grady lifts a finger my way—"I just saw the email you sent about the new gazebo that's being delivered. Great idea."

"*Brilliant* idea," Nessa adds. "A gazebo overlooking the bluff? Couples will be lining up to use it as a wedding venue. Consider the inn booked into the foreseeable future."

"That's what I like to hear. And thanks for watching the front desk, Grady. I won't be long," I say as I head on over to the ballroom with Nessa.

I've been the manager here at the inn for years now and I consider it my baby. It's actually owned by a wealthy earl in England, but he has little to nothing to do with it. I've fallen in love with this expansive mansion whose grounds cover acres and acres. Outside of the inn there are over three dozen cottages that dot the vicinity and I happen to live in one. Jasper lives right in front of me and I rather like the proximity.

Nessa giggles as we come upon the entry to the saucy soiree.

"I can't believe you got Fish and Sherlock to sit at the door like that. There's not a soul who's passed by that can resist them," she says as she heads on into the venue without me.

A giggle rides up my own throat at the sight of the adorable twosome.

Fish happens to be the stray kitten I found and fell in love with almost a year ago. She's a black and white longhaired tabby who is both witty and sharp as a whip. And Sherlock Bones is a red and white freckled mixed-breed pup that happens to belong to Jasper. Thankfully, Fish and Sherlock seem to get along fine—for the most part.

Fish lets out a yowl. ***Whose idea was this light up collar?***

My lips curve with a private smile. There certainly is a perk to hearing people's thoughts—I can hear the thoughts of animals, too. And believe me when I say, nine times out of ten I'd rather listen to what they have to say instead of my human counterparts.

Fish wraps herself around my ankles. ***I'm going to dream in pink and red, Bizzy. And we both know if I don't have a good night's rest, neither will you.***

"Good Lord, nothing is truer than that," I whisper. Especially considering the fact she sleeps right on top of my head on most nights.

I pick her up and offer a quick kiss just above her nose.

"How about one more hour and then I'll take you straight home and give you an extra helping of dinner?"

She purrs as loud as a jet engine. **The things I do for love.**

"And for your Fancy Beast cat food," I whisper as I land her back to the ground.

Sherlock gives a little bark. I'm not sure how, but they seem to understand one another just fine. Sherlock has a bright red bow around his neck and looks every bit the special gift he is.

I don't mind staying, Bizzy, Sherlock howls. **And I don't mind the bow, either. I know you'll more than bacon up for it.**

I'd correct him on his grammar, but we all know he's right. With some pets, their currency is love. With Sherlock, it is very much bacon.

"You bet," I say before giving him a quick pat between the ears. I'm about to head on in when Fish jumps in my path.

One more thing, Bizzy. Her whiskers twitch. **I have a very dark feeling about tonight. I don't know why, but I feel as if something sinister is afoot.**

"A dark feeling?" I whisper.

I'm about to reassure her everything will be just fine when I pick up an errant internal voice.

It's happening. And it's happening tonight. And once they're gone, I won't have a single problem in the world.

I straighten and quickly scan the area, but the crowd is so thick it could have come from anyone. I try my hardest to look directly at the crowd and try to pry into their minds, but most of them are mentally sizing one another up, wondering when the night will end and whether they'll end it alone.

I knew I'd be a lot of things... The voice goes off once again and I'm having a hard time deciphering if it's from a man or a woman. Unless they're standing right in front of me, they sound more or less monotone. *But I never thought I'd have the nerve to eliminate someone from the planet. I guess that will make me a killer.*

My heart seizes as I look into the sea of people congregating in the ballroom.

Fish is right. Something sinister is afoot, and unless it's stopped, it just might mean murder.

2

The ballroom at the Country Cottage Inn is glammed up and ready for its close-up with Cupid. Despite the fact I've spent the majority of the day helping with the decorations, the sight of all the love-inspired grandeur takes my breath away.

An entire sea of white twinkle lights is strung up above. The chandeliers that dot the cavernous ceiling are dimmed just enough to give the place a romantic appeal, there are long-stemmed red roses on the refreshment tables, and everywhere you look there are pink and white metallic heart-shaped balloons.

I spot my best friend, Emmie Crosby, across the room, and I'm about to head that way when a mop of gray hair in a red sequin kaftan accosts me.

"Georgie." I laugh as her firm embrace keeps me from falling.

"Bizzy Baker, you've outdone yourself." She holds out a hand to the crowd of couples who are mingling and laughing while soft rock music plays through the speakers. "The photo booth is a hit. And nice touch having riding crops and fuzzy pink handcuffs as parting gifts."

"What?" I squawk in horror. "I would never have handcuffs and riding crops as parting gifts." I scan the area and, sure enough, I spot a handful of women playfully swatting away at their partners. "Elvis must have brought them." I'm not sure I would have okayed the event had I known there would be a decidedly naughty slant to the evening. Heck, I wouldn't have invited my own mother to participate.

Speaking of which, I spot her over at the refreshment table loading up on the sweetheart punch. Hopefully, she's not the one spiking it. Although I wouldn't put it past her.

Georgie waves it off. "Elvis said he had nothing to do with those kinky *trinkies*. He thought it was a nice touch from the venue. Besides, we can't put those fuzzy handcuffs back in the can. Macy is out there giving them away as we speak."

"Macy." I close my eyes at the mention of my sassy big sis. "Never mind. I know exactly how those handcuffs and riding crops ended up here."

And just like that, my blonde sister pops up with a knowing smile spread over her face.

"You owe me three hundred dollars." She gives a sly wink. "These naughty little bobbles didn't come cheap, you know."

Macy is older than me by a year. She's chosen to dye her dark hair blonde and wears it in a long bob around the base of her neck. She has pretty blue eyes, and each one sparkles with its own special brand of mischief. She owns a soap and candle shop just down the way on Main Street called Lather and Light. It's not the be-all and end-all for her, but it spits out a shiny dollar now and again, thus keeping her content enough to live in Cider Cove at the moment.

Macy winks over at me. "Don't worry, little sis. I've got you and the big, bad detective covered. You can take home the surplus. That way, the two of you can play good cop, bad cop all night long."

Georgie howls with approval. And I won't lie, there's a naughty part of me that wholeheartedly approves, too.

Macy glances around the vicinity. "Where is Detective Wilder, anyway? I'd keep tabs on him at an event like this. He's a hot commodity and he's not wearing a wedding ring. I'm sorry, Bizzy, but he's still fair game."

I'd roll my eyes if a tiny part of me didn't believe it was true.

"He's out helping his mother check on the progress of her condo."

"Bizzy!" Emmie runs up and offers me an impromptu hug. Emmie Crosby has been my best friend ever since preschool. We share the same dark wavy hair that hits just below our shoulders and same icy blue eyes. In fact, we share the same first name, too—Elizabeth, thus we've each opted to go with the nicknames our families have given us.

"Bizzy. The men are h-o-t!" She gives a little hop, a daring feat in that tight pink dress she's wearing.

Georgie taps her elbow to Emmie's side. "Yeah. And rumor has it, they can s-p-e-l-l, too." She wrinkles her nose at my bestie. "Hey, wait a minute. I thought you were dating one of those h-o-t Wilder brothers?"

It's true. Emmie was dating Jasper's brother, Jamison, for all of a hot Wilder minute. It's a trend Macy started when she decided to date *two* of Jasper's brothers virtually back to back, Jamison *and* Dalton. But after she gave them the old college try—and I mean that in the drunken sorority girl party sense—she unceremoniously dumped them.

Of course, Emmie was more than eager to pick up one of Macy's leftovers, but she and Jamison have been hit-or-miss ever since. And don't get me started on Jasper's brother, Maximus. He not only owns a hot piece of real estate out in Seaview, a trendy restaurant that bears his moniker, but he owned my mother's heart for a few solid weeks, too. Thankfully, they've decided to part ways. I'll admit, it was a wee bit horrifying hearing all the heated stories Georgie pulled out of her. I'm all for my mother finding love and engaging in many more horrifying heated adventures so long as they take place outside of the Wilder family ecosystem.

Emmie shakes her head. "Nope. Jamison and I have taken a step back." She shrugs my way. "It looks as if you're the only one having a wild Wilder time." She leans in. "Please tell me you're having a wild time. That man is a god among men."

Macy offers a mischievous grin my way. "I've got just the thing to assure you have a wild time," she says, plucking the riding crop out of the basket and handing it to me. "And on that note, I have to get back to work. I'm the self-appointed Valentine's fairy."

"I thought that was Cupid's job," Emmie calls out as my sister gets right back to distributing her naughty knickknacks.

"Cupid's stupid!" Macy shoots back, and at least ten different people laugh and raise their glasses full of sweetheart punch as if toasting the notion.

Speaking of things we're serving.

"Emmie," I say, glancing back at the dessert table. "Those raspberry cheesecake bites look amazing. Remind me to give you a raise." Emmie is the manager of the Country Cottage Café and she also happens to be the head baker.

You would think that since *Baker* is actually my surname, I might be pretty decent at wielding a whisk, but the opposite is true. As much as I long to create a scrumptious dessert that's more than mildly palatable, I burn everything I touch in the kitchen. And no matter how hard Emmie has tried to teach me her Zen cooking ways, I find a way to turn even the simplest baking task into a marked disaster.

Ironically, it's the only thing I long to do—bake something edible that, for once, doesn't send someone to the emergency room. Although, in my defense, that was just once and my mother is just fine.

"I'll take the raise." Emmie gives a little hop on the balls of her feet. "I'd better bring out the reserves. They're going fast." She takes off and Georgie elbows me in the ribs.

"You know what else is going fast?" She furrows her gray brows my way. "Your relationship with that vampire you're seeing."

The vampire in question would be Jasper.

Emmie and I might have started the trend of referring to Jasper as a vampire, albeit innocently enough. It stemmed from our love of a book series that centered on sexy undead night dwellers, and well, Georgie is slow to let the supernatural reference die.

Not that I mind. Jasper makes one heck of a hot vampire, and I'd be lying if I didn't admit to looking forward to those neck bites he doles out on the regular.

I wince her way. "Would you think less of me if I confessed that Jasper and I weren't moving fast at all?" It's true. In fact, we're moving at a glacial pace. If we move any slower, we'll have to reintroduce ourselves.

Georgie narrows her gaze over me. "I wouldn't only think less of you, Bizzy Baker, I'd be *wildly* disappointed. See what I did there?" She elbows me again. "See that? See that?"

Before I can say a word in response, Elvis Hendrix himself steps into our midst. Elvis is about my father's age, maybe early sixties, has a full head of dark hair and deep-welled laugh lines when he smiles. There's a loveable quality to him in general, aside from his cheesy moniker, and people seem to gravitate to both him and his app—as evidenced by the outrageous turnout here tonight.

"Elvis." I offer a cheery smile. "Can you believe this crowd? I guess Cupid has his work cut out for himself."

He belts out a warm laugh. "If I have my way, he'll be out of a job. I aim to please." He pulls Georgie's hand forward and kisses the back of it.

I don't know if I should coo or puke. And just before I can decide which way my emotions want to run, Elvis flags someone down as a younger man about my age flashes a toothy grin as he leads an older woman this way.

"Well, look who finally decided to show." Elvis pulls the young man in and offers him a slap on the back.

It's only then I notice the adorable coffee-colored curly-haired puppy in his arms.

Georgie and I break out into a choir of admiration for the tiny little sweet potato.

Believe me, I'd much rather coo for the furry little angel than I would over the fact Elvis here aims to please Georgie with his hand-kissing innuendos. I don't object to the fact he's younger than her; I object to the fact he's weirder than her. And with Georgie that's hard to do. I love her weird—his weird? It *weirds* me out just a little too much.

The younger man bounces the dog in his arms.

"This is Cinnamon," he says. "She's the newest addition to my household. A friend of mine had a litter of labradoodles and I took the runt of the bunch. Don't tell her, though. I think she's perfect."

The tiny pup lets out what sounds like a groan. *If I had a biscuit for every time he says that joke, I'd have a box full of biscuits. And I'd prefer them to his jokes.*

I bite down on a smile. She's just so cute I can't stand it. I'll make sure to dig up a dog treat for her before the night is through.

Georgie claps her hands. "Come on, don't forget to introduce your mother." She gives a wink to the older woman standing next to the man holding the dog. "They think they can forget about us just because we've ripened. But once we hit the dance floor, we'll show these ageist elitists. Ain't that right, toots?" Georgie bucks her hip into the woman's thigh, and Dear God Almighty if it wasn't a power thrust liable to break a pelvic girdle or two.

Elvis gives an odd little grimace. "Georgie, this is my co-designer of the app, Lad Warner, and his fiancée, Emily Carter."

Oh my stars above Cider Cove.

If ever there were a good time for the earth to have one of those spontaneous sinkhole moments, it would be now. There just isn't an elegant way to come back from that granny-based faux pas. Georgie didn't just put her foot into her mouth. She somehow managed to invert her entire body.

Emily Carter is a tall woman, unafraid to stand erect, with short silver-blonde hair and a series of soft lines around her eyes as she pulls a tight smile with her cardinal-colored lips.

"Don't worry. I'm not easily offended." She nods to Georgie. "And since Lad doesn't like to dance, I'll take you up on the offer. I agree. We need to show these ageists what we're capable of." *Or kill them—Lad specifically for not defending me.*

My mouth falls open because innately I know I need to say something—something clever perhaps—but the only thing that's currently emitting from me is a steady series of choking noises.

Cinnamon yelps and squirms.

"Here, let me," I say, quickly taking the puppy into my arms. "Oh, you're so soft. I just love you." She gives my face a quick lick and a squeal of a laugh evicts from me. "I think we're going to be good friends." I look up at Lad and smile. "So you helped develop the app?"

He winces. "You could say I'm the brawn. Elvis is the brain."

Elvis rocks back on his heels with the accolade. *If by brawn, he means dead weight, then he's got that right.*

Emily nods to Lad. "And I might just invest in the app myself. I'm here to see what all the excitement is about. I have no use for the app itself since Cupid has already done his dirty work on me."

She holds up a sizable engagement ring and Georgie and I gasp at its sheer girth.

I offer Emily an approving nod. Good on her for finding a decent man to spend the rest of her life with. Who cares about the age difference? Nobody batted a lash when my father married that twenty-two-year-old a few years back. With the exception of my mother, of course. And I do believe there was a *bat* involved in there somewhere—it got her banned from the wedding, too. Typically, my mother attends those splashy soirees that feature my father. She always says it's a great way to have a free meal with her children. She isn't wrong.

Emily winks at Georgie. "We're still capable of plenty. What do you do, Georgie?"

Georgie nods. "I'm an artist who specializes in mosaics. I'm reconstructing the face of Main Street, right here in Cider Cove. Just because we're over eighty doesn't mean we need to curl up and knit." She winces before leaning my way. "Which reminds me, I'm all out of that skein of lavender yarn I'm using to make your wedding blanket."

"I didn't know you knew how to knit," I say.

"I don't, but I figure by the time you get hitched I'll have plenty of time to master the art."

"Thank you, I think." Why do I feel as if there was a slight in there somewhere?

I turn to Emily. "I'm Bizzy Baker, and this is my friend, Georgie Conner. I'm the manager here at the inn."

Emily's brows rise a notch. "That's wonderful. I happen to own the Carter Art Centers. If you ever want to hold a class here at the inn for your guests, I would love to send over an instructor or two."

I take a quick breath. "Carter Art Centers? Wow, you've got a center in just about every other town. Hey! You do those couples' classes, don't you? The sip and paint and those spicy drawing classes? You're really big."

A soft laugh bubbles from her. "That's right. We've just opened our fiftieth store, and we're franchising nationally as well."

Lad wraps an arm around her waist. "Carter Industries is looking to hit the three million dollar mark in sales this year."

Elvis bucks. "You're sweeping the nation. Congratulations." Another crowd moves in through the door and Elvis looks that way. "Excuse me. I'd better get out there and make sure things are moving and grooving in the right direction." He takes off swiftly.

"If you don't mind"— Lad looks back at the crowd himself and does a double take—"I'd better do the same."
Great. It's all about timing, and Colt has none.

He takes off with a marked look of anger on his face.

Emily nods. "I'm off to the little girls' room to powder my nose." **And maybe hike my skirt a notch or two. I may be a woman of a certain age, but I'm not** *afraid of a little leg. And by the looks of it, neither is any other woman in this room. Except for Paige, of course. It would kill her to show a little skin.*

No sooner does she leave than the woman I saw earlier strides after Emily.

"Oh," I say. "I totally forgot there was a woman asking to see Lad. Oh well." I shrug over at Georgie. "She's found Emily. That's close enough."

Both Emily and the young woman begin to argue and bicker right there in the middle of the room.

I glance to the door and spot Lad talking to a man in a dark suit, neatly trimmed hair, and their conversation looks rather heated, too. Lad gets right in his face before giving the man a hard shove to the chest, and I give Cinnamon a protective squeeze.

Lad turns and assesses the room until he spots Emily going at it with the younger woman and his features harden as if he were fit to kill.

Something tells me tonight will have more hostility than it ever will love.

And if we're not careful, Cider Cove just might have another homicide on its hands, too. I head over to the dueling divas just as the lights dim a notch and the music grows livelier. A disco ball begins to spin overhead and sprays the room with metallic pink and red beams of fragmented light.

"Excuse me, ladies." I raise my voice just enough for them to hear me, and then a touch louder than that so they know I mean business. My hand lies protectively over the shivering pooch in my arms, trying my best to assure her she's not the one in trouble here. "Is there something I can help you with?" I look to the two blondes and their resemblance is striking.

"Bizzy"—Emily leans in—"this is my daughter, Paige."

I straighten and force a smile.

Her daughter? Isn't this the same woman who was internally threatening to kill someone when she barreled into the place? I try to rewind my mind, but the music and the lights are making me feel dizzy. Wait, wasn't that someone *Lad*?

"Nice to meet you." I wrinkle my nose. "Actually, I think we met at the reception counter. Did you find who you were looking for?" I don't dare say Lad's name.

She gives a reluctant nod. ***No, but I will soon enough.***

I glance to the door where I saw Lad last, the man Paige was asking for to begin with. I fully expect to see him in a full-blown brawl, but instead the man with the dark suit and neatly trimmed hair is near the refreshment table helping himself to Emmie's raspberry cheesecake bites, and right about now, he's the smartest person in the room.

Not too far from him stands my mother with her feathered hair, her popped collar, and overall preppy appeal. If Ree Baker is anything, she's a true-blue throwback to the eighties. She's cuttingly beautiful, ageless in the most literal sense, and a strong woman in every capacity. The men here should be just a little afraid of her. Lord knows I am.

I scan the back wall until I spot Lad cornering a redhead. She's considerably shorter than he is and looks to be wearing a raincoat.

"It was nice meeting you, Paige," I say. "I hope you both have a great time."

I take off into the bustling crowd until I hit the back of the room, but both Lad and the redhead are gone.

I'm about to head out into the main hall to get some respite from the noise when a short brunette in a neon green dress strides up and gives Cinnamon a warm pat on the back.

Boy, that chartreuse number she has on is one way to differentiate yourself from a sea of little black dresses.

"Hey there, cutie pie." She gives the dog a kiss on one of its fuzzy floppy ears. *If you're here, that means he's here, and we are back in business, baby. Or at least we will be, if I have my way.*

She offers me an amicable smile. Her nose is wide and prominent, her cheeks high-cut, and she has a squirrely look in her eyes as if you couldn't quite trust her.

"So, where's the dog's owner?" She bats her lashes up at me as if she were trying to pull a fast one.

"Lad?" I try to act as if I didn't just pry into her inner diatribe. "If he's smart, he's at the dessert table." I nod that way and she's off to the races.

I tuck my lips near the puppy's ear. "Your daddy just might be the most popular person in the room."

Cinnamon gives a moan that sounds like a tiny laugh. *That man never has a free moment. In fact, I was hoping to get to know him better tonight myself.*

A tiny laugh bubbles from me. "I know this comes as a surprise, but I can hear your thoughts and understand them, too."

Cinnamon gives a sharp bark. *Really? I didn't think anyone could understand what I was saying, let alone thinking.*

"Well, I can—and believe me when I say, I'm thrilled to communicate with you. I much prefer speaking to pets than some people. And as for you getting to spend time with Lad tonight, I think you'll have to get in line, Cinnamon. And I have a feeling it's a very long line."

He seems quite nice when he's not busy arguing with someone. I think arguing is one of his favorite pastimes.

I have a feeling she's right. Between Paige's anger toward him and his shoving match with the man in the suit, I'd say Lad has more than a few issues on his plate.

An hour races by.

Jasper just texted to let me know he just got back to his cottage and would be at the inn soon enough. And being the official president of the Jasper Wilder Fan Club, I decide to head out to the front of the inn to intercept him with a kiss before we get tangled up in this singles-mingles madness. This group date with Cupid is turning into one big rowdy party, with both my mother and Georgie leading the pack on the dance floor.

I head out one of the side exits that leads to an overgrown fountain sitting to the left of the inn.

The Country Cottage Inn is a two-story structure covered in ivy. There's a blue, stone cobbled path that leads around the building and circles all the way to a white sandy beach. The Country Cottage Café is attached to the ocean side of the inn as well and boasts of expansive views of the Atlantic from its sunroom.

The icy air hits me as soon as I step out into the clear starry night. The scent of night jasmine perfumes the vicinity as I take in the peace and calm the outdoors bring, compared to the riot going on inside.

A three-tiered fountain stands prominent before me. It's at least ten feet of verdigris copper, and the water raining down from tier to tier is backlit a gorgeous shade of cobalt. The sound of its trickling is a welcome relief to my tired ears.

Cinnamon begins to whimper and squirm, so I let her down and she heads off for the grass nearby to do her business. And as I straighten from the effort, something metallic catches my eyes near the cobbled path that leads to the parking lot.

"What the..." I head on over and seize in horror at what I find.

A gun sits abandoned, gleaming in the moonlight as if kissed by the stars itself to showcase its danger. Instinctually, I pick it up. The metal is so cold, it shocks the flesh on the palm of my hand.

I turn toward the inn and take a breath.

I'll need to take this to Jasper.

My feet start in that direction, and just as I'm about to come upon the fountain, I see it, or rather *him*.

Lying partially in the fountain itself is a man who looks as if he's fallen backward into the pool of water. His legs are hooked over the side as he floats on his back, his arms spread wide. The bright pink imprint of a kiss stains the side of his cheek, his last kiss. There's a dark crimson stain in the middle of his chest, and to my fright his eyes remain wide open as he stares vacantly into the sky.

"Bizzy?" Jasper calls out in a warm voice as he jogs on over, his feet slowing as he observes my hand cradling the gun, the body in the fountain.

But it's not just any body. It's Lad. And he won't be arguing with anyone else ever again.

Lad Warner is dead.

3

"Bizzy?" Jasper searches me with wild eyes as he flicks his fingers. "Give me the gun."

I do so willingly, and he quickly heads over to poor Lad and checks for a pulse.

"He's gone," he pants as he pulls out his phone and calls for backup.

"What the hell happened?" he asks, heading my way. His eyes still wide with fright as if I might have actually had something to do with the malfeasance.

"I don't know. I didn't hear or see a thing. I was just coming out here to meet you. I put the dog down and that's when I saw the gun. I picked it up and I was headed to find you and that's when I saw him lying there." I glance back at Lad and my chest bucks with emotion. "Oh dear God, he's really dead."

Jasper pulls me in and I take in the heady scent of his cologne.

Jasper is a six-foot-two wall of muscles, typically disguised behind a well-tailored suit. He looks comely to a fault tonight and, to be fair, every night, with his jet-black hair and silver-gray eyes that make every woman in the vicinity—in the great state of Maine—sit up for attention. And as much as I'd like to be doing just that here, he is comforting me. There's been another body, another murder, and that means another killer is on the loose.

I pull back and soak up every inch of the man I love—of that man who still doesn't have a clue about the fact I can read minds, and sadly I was about to fix that later tonight.

"I'm a suspect, aren't I?" I ask, sullen at the thought.

"Just in theory." He winces. "I'm sorry, Bizzy. It's just protocol."

In less than a moment, the area is swarming with sheriff's deputies as cruisers with their lights flashing pull up on the scene.

Deputy Leo Granger jogs out of the side door of the inn, pausing a moment to pick up Cinnamon.

"What's going on?" he asks as he cranes his neck to look past us at the cluster of deputies. "Where's the emergency?" He spots Lad in the fountain and groans. "Not again."

"Again," I say, taking the poor shivering pooch from him. "Don't look, Cinnamon," I whisper, and she buries her face in my chest.

Don't worry, Bizzy. I don't want to see it. I heard everything. How does this happen? How does a perfectly healthy man fall into a fountain? Am I going back to my mother now? Oh, she was so certain I'd do well in my new home. I'd hate to disappoint her.

"You can stay with me." I give her furry face a quick kiss before shrugging up at both Jasper and Leo. "She's frightened. I want to make her feel better." I wrinkle my nose at Leo. "By the way, I'm a suspect."

Jasper nods. "I found Bizzy holding what I presume is the murder weapon." He glances down at the gun in his hand before removing a plastic bag from his pocket and sealing it inside. "There might be hope of finding a third print on it." He sighs my way. "Don't leave town." He offers a wry smile. "Leo, why don't you put the inn on lockdown? I want everyone's name and a contact number before they're dismissed. Bizzy, make sure they leave through the east exit. I'm cordoning off the area, and since we're so close to the entry that means the front doors, too."

"Sure thing," I say. "And I'll take care of Sherlock." I hike up on the balls of my feet and give him a quick kiss on the lips.

Jasper manufactures a short-lived, albeit bleak, smile. *My girlfriend, the suspect. This is going to go over well at the precinct. I'd better clear her, and quick. But of all the things to be holding, Bizzy had to find the murder weapon. And what are the odds of her finding every single body that's turned up in the last few months?*

His lips curve my way once again, this time no smile. *My girlfriend the serial killer. Now that would be a new one.*

I'm about to swat him when Leo wraps an arm around me and leads me to the side while Jasper gets right to work doing what he does best—suspecting me of slaughtering the masses.

A dark laugh hums through Leo.

"Come on, Biz. Give the guy a break. Those were his personal thoughts. You can't lambaste him for it."

Leo Granger can pry into other people's thoughts with the best of them. He's the one that told me that we fall under a class of people who hold this same quirky talent. We're what's known as transmundane, further classified as telesensual, which basically means we've gone pro with the mind reading gig.

I'm not sure how Leo came about his rare supernatural talent, but as for me, it all stems back to that Halloween party when I was thirteen. It was the night

Mackenzie Woods saw fit to shove me underwater in a whiskey barrel prepped for a game of bobbing for apples.

Four things came from that horrific day. One: I have an irrational fear of large bodies of water. And truth be told, I find my own bathtub a bit too dicey for me. Two: I'm petrified of confined spaces. Three: It initiated an intense distrust of Mack Woods, who now holds a quasi-powerful political position as the town's mayor. And last, but not least, four: It inadvertently turned me into the town's nosiest resident—the girl who could read minds. It's not a title I was looking for.

I glance back to Jasper. "I'll give him a break, Leo. I just hope he gives me a break. I'm ready to do it. I'm ready to tell him my little secret." I nod to Leo. "And if you're ready, you can tell him yours, too."

Leo rocks back on his heels, but before he can answer, a whirlwind of a woman appears in our midst.

"Camila." Leo gives a wistful shake of the head. "You've got timing, I'll give you that."

Camila Ryder is tall, vexingly beautiful, with warm chestnut hair that rides down her back in waves. Her skin is tawny and her lips are perfectly full. But for as stunning as she is, she is just that wicked. She once dated Jasper. Come to find out, they were briefly engaged, and shortly thereafter she made the decision to ditch Jasper for his best friend Leo Granger. And that's exactly why Jasper doesn't want anything to do with either of them.

"What are you doing here?" I hiss her way. When Leo and Camila were dating, she somehow got it out of him that he could read minds. And after coming to Cider Cove, she discovered that I could, too. In an effort to tear Jasper and me apart, she called the feds in to report supernatural activity in the area—with me as ground zero. Thankfully, Mackenzie—yes, Mayor Woods, my previous nemesis—thought Camila was out to steal back Leo and she wasn't having it. Mack stooped low in an effort to get rid of Camila by way of turning the feds right back in the wily wench's direction.

Camila takes a deep breath. "I'm here looking for love, Bizzy. I subscribe to Elvis Hendrix's service. The Dependable app is having a mixer, and I came ready to mingle with Cupid." She glances over my shoulder and I follow her gaze to Jasper.

I can't help but note Camila looks starry-eyed at the sight of him.

"You can go home now," I say. "Cupid has left the building. And Jasper is already taken in the event you've forgotten."

Mackenzie strides up. "And so is Leo." Mackenzie looks like a sin in the tiny red dress she's poured herself into. Her dark hair is swept up into a chignon and her lips are the same cherry shade as her frock. "Rumor has it, Cupid went back to Sheffield. That is where you're from, isn't it?"

"*Was.*" She nods. "I'm in Seaview now. Within walking distance to my new employer, the Seaview Sherriff's Department." She runs her finger down the front of Leo's tie. "I'll see you at work, big boy." She gives a slow wink before slinking right off the property.

"She probably did it," I say. "I hope." There are a lot of things wrong with Camila Ryder, but it's nothing a good life sentence couldn't fix.

Mackenzie leans my way. "Speaking of doing it, I need the Country Cottage Café to cater the Valentine's dance at the community center on the fourteenth. Our slogan this year is *Cider Cove, a place to hang your heart.*"

"Sounds...interesting. Cute, I think? I'm sorry. My head's all over the place. Of course, we'll cater."

I quickly put a text into both Nessa and Grady, letting them know what happened and where to direct traffic as far as the exit is concerned.

Leo heads back into the inn to help collect the contact information he needs, and I head back in along with him, only to be accosted by my mother and Georgie.

"What's going on, Bizzy?" My mom doesn't waste any time in scooping Cinnamon out of my arms and cradling the tiny angel herself.

Georgie leans in. "Is it true? Has there been another murder?"

My lips press tight. "Yes. And the victim was Lad, the owner of this poor sweet treat." I give Cinnamon's back a quick stroke.

Mom hands her back to me. "We need to get out of here, Georgie. I'm spending the night with you. I hope you have room on that futon in the living room. I don't want to drive all the way home alone. My cats won't even notice I'm gone."

Mom adopted a pair of sweet kittens last Christmas named Mistletoe and Holly. My brother thought they were the perfect crazy cat lady starter kit, and I still giggle when I think of his comment.

Georgie links her arm through my mother's. "I've always got room for an uptight prima donna that's vowed to get to the bottom of my baby girl's imprisonment."

Mom gives a prolonged blink my way. "Bizzy, Georgie's daughter, Juni, is in prison and Georgie doesn't know why. Do you think Jasper can help us get to the bottom of this?"

"Absolutely," I say. "We'll try tomorrow."

Georgie gives a frenetic nod. "Thanks, Bizzy. But no hurry. According to the email she sent, she's having a great time. Juni's in the middle of a love triangle with two of the guards and she's anxious to see how it will all play out." She makes a face as she looks around the ballroom. "Too bad *we* didn't have such a great time. So much for Cupid's arrow striking gold. I didn't have any luck with the men."

I tip my head. "I thought you were seeing Elvis?"

"I'm not now that he's a suspect." She narrows her eyes over at mine. "And you know he is, Bizzy. It wouldn't surprise me at all if he were guilty as sin. That boy has a naughty streak a mile wide." She turns to my mother. "How'd you fare, Prep?"

My mother rolls her eyes. "Two different men asked if I wanted to watch Netflix and chill. As if I'd want to waste a perfectly good night falling asleep while watching TV. I could have done that alone. It's too bad. They were both real lookers, too. I would have taken them up on a saucier offer."

They take off and I don't bother correcting my mother on the intentions of those men who proposed the raunchy idea to begin with.

I'm about to head into the crowd when I spot the friendly brunette who was petting Cinnamon earlier and asking where her owner was. The woman's bright green dress glows under the duress of the twinkle lights like a homing beacon.

She staggers my way, dazed.

"Hey," I say in my sweetest voice. "Are you okay?"

"I'm fine." She gives a hard blink. "I'm just a little shaken, that's all. I heard that a man I knew was killed." *Dead as a doornail. My life will never be the same. And if I don't leave soon, it will be changed forever.* "I'm sorry. I have to go."

"You can't go," I say, quickly blocking her path, using poor Cinnamon as an inadvertent shield. "I'll have to get your name and... occupation. My name is Bizzy, and I run the inn."

She takes a quick breath as she sizes me up. "I'm Madeline Harper. I run the night classes at the Carter Art Center in Edison."

I make a face without meaning to. Nothing good ever happens in Edison. She's practically guilty by association of where she works the nightshift. Now it's my turn to run my eyes up and down her person, and something on her knee catches my attention.

"Is that a grass stain?" I say, looking down as she gives her leg a quick pat.

"I tripped over a sprinkler head on the way in. You should really have them lowered. You're lucky I don't sue."

I blink back with surprise. "How well did you know Lad? I mean, I'm assuming you met him through his fiancée since you work for her company."

The girl flinches when I mention Emily.

**Rub it in, why don't you? I hate that old hag.
She should go next.**

"Yes, that's exactly how I met him." She takes off for the crowd headed to the back of the ballroom.

"You'll have to leave your number with the deputy on your way out." I raise my voice just a notch. She just might have done it. And if she did, Emily might be next.

Speaking of Emily, I spot her with her daughter by the refreshment table and they're both noshing on those delectable raspberry cheesecake bites.

Odd. But I suppose people grieve in different ways. Typically, a person goes into shock once they hear news like this and they can't eat for days. But then, some people eat their feelings. And face it, there aren't a lot of things that cheesecake can't make better.

"Emily," I say as I come upon the two of them. "Are you aware of what happened?"

She glances to the ceiling. "Lad is dead." She lets out a horrid moan. "And they won't let me leave or see him." **I've seen enough, but I've got to put on a show. I'll save my anger for when I get home. Although, a bullet to the chest does wonders to quell the rage. It was a good shot. A kill shot they call it.**

My mouth falls open. And to think I was about to ask if she wanted to take Cinnamon home.

Instead, I hold the tiny peanut just a little bit tighter.

Paige offers a weak smile. "I'm not feeling well. I think I might pass out."

I quickly procure a chair for her and a glass of water.

"Thank you," she whispers. ***Now if I can fake my way home, I might just be home free.***

"Oh my goodness," I mutter to myself, but both Emily and Paige look my way. "It just occurred to me that one of you might have been the last to see him alive." I shrug. "You know, before the killer found him." Unless, of course, I'm looking at the killer. Both of them sound guilty enough to me.

Emily and Paige exchange a quick glance.

Emily clears her throat. "Would you mind getting me a glass of water as well, while I try to remember?"

"Sure thing." I take off for the refreshment table and spot the man in the suit that Lad was having it out with. He's talking to the redhead that I saw Lad with earlier.

It's as if some invisible force were moving me in their direction and I can't seem to stop myself.

"Hello," I say. "I'm Bizzy Baker. I run the inn. I'm just going around to all of the guests here tonight and seeing how they're faring."

"Terrible," says the redhead before she offers a short-lived smile my way. Her lipstick looks smudged. Her mascara does, too. "I'd better get going. I have an early shift tomorrow." She glances at her phone for the time.

"Oh?" I lean in. "Where do you work?"

Her gaze falls to Cinnamon a moment and I try to pry into her mind, but it's all white fuzz. Usually it's indicative of inappropriate thoughts, but at times like these, shock can set it off as well.

"I'm sorry. I work at a bookshop in Seaview. I have a shipment of new releases and I need to stock the floor." She gives the man in the suit a hard look. "Goodnight, Colt. Don't let the bedbugs bite."

That was an odd thing to say.

The man in the suit, *Colt*, glowers at her a moment.

"Goodnight, Natalie," he growls it out. "I'd say the same, but I'm not feeling so generous. Not even tonight." *God, especially not tonight.* He turns my way. "I'm sorry, Bizzy. I'll need to make a few phone calls. Lad and I were once related. My aunt married his uncle. The family is going to be a mess." *I'll be fine. If there was anyone who was better off dead, it was Lad. Poor guy. He should have seen this coming.*

He starts to take off and I pull him back by the sleeve. "Um, the girl, I didn't get her name."

He glances in the general direction she took off in.

"Natalie Weiland." He shakes his head. *She's been nothing but a bag full of trouble from start to finish. And yet, a part of me still wishes she and Lad were still together. Those were simpler times.*

Hell, I wish that I were still with Nat. Those were even better times. "You had a nice party here tonight." He nods as he takes a step away. *Too bad Lad had to go and ruin it.*

"What was your last name? And your occupation?" I ask, hoping he'll take the same bait.

"Ferguson." He frowns into the crowd. "I work for a bank." He takes off into the crowd and it's just Cinnamon and me as the inner voices of those around us begin to fill my head.

Lad Warner bit the big one.

A bullet to the chest.

Some might say he deserved to die. I would be one of them.

He's gone. And now I have to live with his blood on my hands for the rest of my life. Who knew there would be a murder here tonight?

Me.

That's who.

"Did you know there were white chocolate chips tucked inside these luscious raspberry cheesecake bites?" Georgie waves one at me as if she were wielding a threat. Her wiry gray hair surrounds her head like a silver pompom, giving off that freshly electrocuted look this morning. Her baby pink kaftan is rather low-cut and is decorated with tiny red sequin hearts. There's something both charming and alarming about it.

It's the very next day after that awful tragedy, and despite the fact the Country Cottage Café is bustling with guests, outside the window I see dark clouds brewing above the Atlantic.

"I sure do know all about those yummy little nuggets," I say to Emmie who just popped up beside me at the counter. "The white chocolate chips were my bright idea."

Georgie gives an approving wink as she pops another one into her pie hole.

Mom and Georgie just stopped in for breakfast and wisely opted for cheesecake rather than their usual fare.

Mom moans through a bite.

"Bizzy, you must give me the recipe." She gives a few rapid blinks to the ceiling while enjoying the sweet treat. Mom's hair is perfectly petrified in the same feathered style it's been frozen in since 1982. She's donned a lavender sweater with a pink blouse underneath, the collar popped to her ears. That's my mother, Ree Baker, fighting the good preppy fight, three decades strong and counting.

"Who am I kidding?" she grunts. "I'm the one that passed down my bad baking genes your way. I'll just keep dropping by until I weigh a thousand pounds. The cheesecake is worth it. Emmie, you're a genius."

"I don't know about that, but thank you." Emmie laughs as she readjusts her frilly red apron with pink lace trim and heart appliques strewn throughout.

Emmie looks well decorated for the upcoming holiday centered on love, and the café is, too. The groundskeeper, Jordy, who is not only Emmie's brother, but my ex-husband (of less than twenty-four hours. Vegas, an Elvis impersonator, and bad Jim Beam were involved. Need I say more?) has been adhering more metallic hearts to just about every free surface than he'd like to remember. He's in the sunroom at the moment doing just that, and each heart that goes up has me more enamored with my true love, Jasper Wilder. I truly feel as if our relationship is about to take a major turn in the right direction. I can feel it in my creaky bones. And I'm ready for it. More than ready.

"Georgie?" I slide another cheesecake bite her way. "What did Elvis have to say about his business partner being killed?"

She shakes her head. "He's devastated. But he wanted me to tell you he wants to rent out the ballroom for a do-over. He's hoping for next Saturday. He's got a huge fiasco planned." She shudders. "I mean *fiesta*."

Mom grunts, "I think you had it right the first time."

"No problem, Georgie," I say. "It's free and I'll book it for him."

Emmie sucks in a quick breath as she looks my way. "I almost forgot to tell you. Nessa said she saw a brunette with a lime green dress running out of the inn just before you found the body. I bet that's our killer."

"A brunette with a lime green dress?" I blink back. "I saw her speaking to Lad earlier in the evening. But she was back in the ballroom well after he was killed. I spoke with her myself. Her name is Madeline Harper and she works at the art center in Edison."

Mom blinks to the ceiling. "That's her first mistake. Nothing good ever happens in Edison. Did I ever tell you I met your father in Edison?"

"*No*." My mouth rounds out with surprise. "Now see there? Something good *did* happen in Edison."

Georgie lifts a finger while doing her best to inhale yet another raspberry cheesecake bite.

"That's where I last saw Juniper Moonbeam." Her left eye squints heavily. "And now she's in the big house doing the hokey pokey with a bunch of maniacal security guards. For her sake, I hope they're cute. Maybe she can get a boyfriend out of the deal."

Mom shudders. "Trust me, Georgie. Nobody goes to prison hoping to get lucky. In fact, it's quite the opposite. We'll have to find out what she was busted for. And then we'll have to hire an entire legal team to bust her out."

"Mom"—I lean her way—"that's so nice of you to take up Juni's plight. I mean, she was married to Dad and all."

Mom waves me off. "Are you kidding? She's a part of a very exclusive sorority. I don't mind helping an ex-Baker sister out. I'd like to think one of them would do the same for me."

Georgie claps her hands as she looks to the entry. "Here comes the cavalry!"

I look to find my father and Jasper's mother, Gwyneth, headed this way. They've been joined at the hip as of late, and as they should be considering they're engaged.

"Ladies." Dad nods our way before offering me a firm embrace. "Bizzy Bizzy." He's echoed my name for as long as I can remember. Dad has full cheeks and a devilish gleam in his eyes. There's an overall boyish charm about him that women the world over can't seem to resist, thus the record amount of divorces he's survived without being slaughtered.

And Gwyneth is a gorgeous woman with skin as pale as paper, hair as black as night, and lips dipped in the blood of her latest victim. Okay, so she's not that bad. Her glossy black hair is neatly pulled up into a bun and she's donned a navy pantsuit with a magenta scarf tied around her neck. She's always stylish, and *always* speaks her mind.

"Georgie." She bows her head to look over at Georgie from over the top of her glasses. "You've raised a criminal. But I happened to have an uncle who escaped from Alcatraz. With my blood onboard, I'm certain we can free just about any jailbird. She could have slaughtered the judge, but we'll make sure she walks."

The four of them migrate off to the sunroom, murmuring about defense tactics and the vast amounts of money this jailbreak might cost them.

Emmie leans in. "I'd better keep them caffeinated."

"Good idea. Take a tray of those raspberry cheesecake bites with you, too. I have a feeling they'll need a few extra carbs to perform an Alcatraz worthy escape."

"Good thinking." She heads that way just as Macy enters the café, holding both Fish and Cinnamon in her arms.

She lets Fish jump down onto the stool at the bar.

Bizzy, your sister lacks your delicate charm. She's abrasive, rude, and full of bitterness and vinegar. Fish shakes out her fur. *I rather like her.*

"Bizzy Baker." My blonde sassy sis picks up Cinnamon's paw and waves at me. "I swear if you don't give me this dog, I'm going to disown you."

Cinnamon lets out a moan. *She is rather abrasive, rude, and full of bitterness and vinegar. I'm not so sure about this.*

Macy's glossy lips twist as if she understood the curly-haired pooch herself.

She tucks her lips next to the dog's ear. "I eat a steady diet of steak and pizza. And contrary to what that mean old witch standing here says, I like to share."

Fish lets out a riotous roar before shooting my sister the stink eye.

Nobody calls Bizzy a witch but me.

I make a face at Fish before continuing with my sister.

"Cinnamon isn't mine to give away. What's going on, Macy? We both know you're not a pet person." I slide the plate full of raspberry cheesecake bites her way and she quickly, and might I add wisely, snaps one up. "Let me guess. You want to capitalize off Cinnamon's cuteness to drum up business for Lather and Light?"

She squints her disdain over at me. "I'll have you know, business is brisk. I'm having a two-for-one sale on all heart-shaped bath bombs."

"*Ooh*," I coo. "I might stop by myself."

"You won't be able to." She leans in, a smile swimming on her lips. "I know you're off to investigate, and I want in on this good time. Where to now, Bizzy? The midnight review down in Edison? I'm your girl. I'll put away my marvelous morals and watch a bunch of men strutting around in banana hammocks. So feel free to cast Georgie and Emmie to the side." She gives a long blink. "I'll take one for the team."

Emmie hops back to the counter and snatches Fish off the stool in front of her.

"What's going on?" she asks. "Why does Macy look as if she's about to bite into a side of beefcake?"

"Because she's delusional," I tell her. "She thinks I'm bringing her along on my investigation."

Emmie gets that squirrely look in her eyes that usually means she's up to no good, or at least she's hoping to be.

She bites down on her lip. "Where are we going, Biz?"

Macy shoves her elbow to Emmie's side. "I call the strip club."

"I'm not going to a strip club." I pull out my phone and look up the Carter Art Center in Edison. "I'm going to a sip and paint art class tonight at four-thirty. It looks like we'll be working with acrylics."

"What?" Macy snatches the phone from me. "Oh my God, this place boasts of a bottomless glass of vino! There's no way you're evicting me from this."

Emmie peers over her shoulder. "Red or white wine? I'm a chardonnay girl myself. Bizzy, since you don't drink, you can be the designated driver."

I pluck my phone back. "Fine. Just promise you'll keep your nose to the acrylic grindstone and I'll let you tag along."

Macy gives a wry smile. "I'll go as far as pitching for the classes. At least that way, I can still feel like I'm in charge."

I tip my head to the side. "Has anyone ever told you that you have some serious control issues?"

"Only every date I've ever been on. And I'm damn proud of it, too."

A six-foot-two wall of muscles bound in a dark gray suit with an adorable mutt springing by his side strides into the café and casts those dreamy gray eyes my way.

"Jasper's here," I hiss as I take Cinnamon from Macy. "Time to commence Operation Distraction. Sorry," I whisper in the curly pup's ear. "But you're my first line of defense."

I head on over and give Sherlock Bones his morning back scratch.

Thanks, Bizzy. I see Georgie in the sunroom. Is it too late to beg for breakfast?

"You're in luck, Sherlock. There's a run of bacon in the kitchen. I'll have Emmie bring out your breakfast."

He lets out an approving bark. *You're a beautiful soul, Bizzy. And I'll miss you when I'm gone. Jasper has threatened to take me to work with him today.*

My mouth squares out over at Jasper. "Why do I get the feeling you're taking Sherlock to the department today?"

His brows meet in the middle, but there's a smile rising on his lips just for me.

"Because you are one intuitive lady."

I offer him a lingering kiss right over his lips. Jasper's cologne is thick and full-bodied as if it were just applied, and I know for a fact he's fresh from the shower because I can still smell the soap on his skin.

I bat my lashes up at him flirtatiously.

"Hey, hot stuff." I take a page out of Macy's playbook and wave at him with Cinnamon's paw. "What's cooking?"

His brows narrow in like a couple of birds in flight. ***Why do I get the feeling Bizzy's got something cooking?***

"Just ducking out for the day and wanted to do this." He wraps his arms around me and lands another sizzler onto my mouth. "I'm afraid I've got to work late."

I twist my lips. "I guess that axes dinner. And believe me, I'd much rather be with you. But as it turns out, I'll be plenty entertained."

"You will? What's cooking with you?" He pulls back and examines me. ***Yup. There it is. That wild look in her eyes she gets just before she jumps into trouble with both feet.***

My mouth falls open and I can't help but frown at him.

"I'm having drinks with Macy and Emmie later this afternoon." I wrinkle my nose. "But since I don't really drink, I'm sort of the self-appointed designated driver."

His lips part as if he were about to ask the next logical question—*where*, but thankfully, Jordy nods my way and heads over, holding what appears to be several torn pieces of paper pinched between his fingers. Jordy is essentially Emmie in male skin. Dark wavy hair, icy blue eyes, and skin that holds a warm tan all year round. He's a playboy at heart, but as of late he's let Camila Ryder use and abuse him, and he's more than liked it, too.

"Hey, Biz." He nods to Jasper as well.

"Is this about the gazebo?" I ask. "I can hardly wait to get it delivered." My lips twitch as I look to Jasper. "As soon as it arrives, I think we should christen it with a picnic." And a few steamy kisses, but I'm sure Jordy doesn't care to hear it.

Jasper's brows hitch, but before he can respond Jordy shakes his head.

"The gazebo is still on its way." He looks to Jasper as he holds out the shredded paper in his hand. "I'm glad you're here. I found this next to one of the trashcans in the ballroom. The sheriff's department cleared the area, and I thought I'd get around to cleaning the place up. I just thought it was odd." He holds out the colorful shreds for us to inspect. "It's a pamphlet from some resort."

I quickly pull out my phone and take a picture of it.

I can make out a blue sky, a white sandy beach, and a couple holding hands from what I can tell of the bits and pieces. The words *escape today to Tu...* are written on the front.

Jasper pulls a plastic bag from his pocket and carefully encapsulates every last bit.

"Jasper"—I increase my hold on Cinnamon—"do you really think this might be evidence?" I whisper the words in the event I send guests into a frenzy. As much as you would think people would be on edge, there seems to be a morbid interest in all the murders that have overtaken Cider Cove as of late. I've fielded more questions this morning by guests who seemed enthralled by the killings rather than horrified, and that alone horrified *me*.

He grimaces a moment. "I don't know. But I'm just crossing the starting line with the investigation, so I don't think it'll hurt to look at it. I'd better get going." He dots my lips with another quick kiss. "Have fun at the bar." He gives a curious look as I give him another far more lingering kiss.

Why do I get the feeling I won't care for the real story behind this bar hop?

Why do I get the feeling he won't like the fact I can read his mind?

I'll have to make the time to tell Jasper all about my transmundane status. The sooner, the better.

We part ways and I wave as he takes Sherlock and leaves, much to Sherlock's bacon-laced protest.

I am going to have fun tonight, and it just so happens that I'll be having fun with a woman by the name of Madeline Harper.

I wonder what sent her running out of the inn just as Lad was killed, only to return to the ballroom afterwards?

I may not know the answer, but I have a feeling I'm about to find out.

5

The Carter Art Center is located right in the heart of Edison—an odd location if you ask me, what with the gentlemen's clubs, the ladies' review, the pawn shop, and tattoo parlor ensconcing it.

But, nonetheless, that didn't stop an entire horde of women from filling up each and every free workspace available in this brightly lit studio. It's not only light and bright inside, but the walls are all covered with uniform canvases about the size of a refrigerator, and each one depicts a different scene from nature: a waterfall, autumn trees, a beautiful ocean sunset, snowy mountain tops, and so on. And surprisingly, each piece looks good enough to hang in a museum, or in the least my cottage.

Emmie perks to life as soon as we step into the place.

"We're here," she sings. "The investigation squad has descended on the premises."

"Ooh." Macy wiggles her shoulders. "Investigation squad. Sounds official. I like that."

"Would you two keep it down?" I whisper—more like a *hissper*.

"*Bizzy*," Macy hisses right back as we snag the last three spots available down in front. She makes a face my way. "All the good spots in the back are taken because we're late. Now we have to sit up front with the teacher, in what's known as the no-fun zone."

Someone laughs from behind and I'm thrilled to see it's Madeline. Her dark hair is swept back into a ponytail and she looks refreshed and energized, especially compared to the other night.

She looks to Macy. "I promise you, every spot in this room is the fun zone." She waves at the class to garner everyone's attention. "Our sommeliers will be making their rounds. Please know that there is no limit to how much we will pour, but we do ask that you know your limits. In my opinion, this is a three glass class. With the music, the sparkling conversation, and don't forget the *painting*, I can guarantee a good time will be had by all! My name is Madeline Harper, but you can call me Maddie." She steps to the front of the class and picks up a canvas with its back facing toward the crowd. "Tonight, I will be instructing you step by step how to paint this beauty." She spins it around to reveal gorgeous crystal blue waters, a pale sandy beach, and a lavender sky. The entire room *oohs* and *ahhs* at the sight, and half the women in the class decide they want to hop onto the next plane to the Caribbean. Music begins to filter throughout the speakers, and the sommeliers begin circulating throughout the room to the delight of the lively crowd.

Emmie leans in. "Hey, Biz"—she whispers as she looks to the suspect in question—"is that her?"

I give a covert nod.

Em makes wild eyes at me. "Do you think she recognizes you?" she whispers just a touch louder, and I'm moved to kick her.

"No, and I want to keep it that way." I glance back over at Madeline and wrinkle my nose. "Maybe she does. But that won't stop me from trying to talk to her. I bet she knows something."

A woman dressed as a waitress comes around and fills Emmie's glass with white wine, Macy's glass with red, and mine with water. I don't mind. I need to keep my head about me. If I get too tipsy, I might be liable to hear the private thoughts of every woman in here at once. It's happened a time or two when I've let my liquor get away from me, thus my desire not to get tipsy.

Madeline calls the class to order once again and instructs us to paint the upper third of our canvases with a base color of lavender.

"While you do that, I'll tell you a little about myself," she volunteers, and I feel like I've hit the jackpot. "I grew up in Rose Glen and went to art school out of state where I majored in frat boys and stale pizza."

A warm laugh circles the room.

"I've always known I was going to do what I love," she continues. "And this, right here, about sums it up." She holds her own paintbrush in the air before getting back to the demonstration model she's working on. "Of course, I also thought I'd be married and have two point five children by now, but here I am, single and not quite ready and willing to mingle."

Another whoop circles the room with some people encouraging her to keep her options open.

"You never know when love will find you," someone shouts.

"It's not all it's cracked up to be!" someone else belts from the back. "Stay single. You'll never have to share the remote!"

More laughter ensues.

"Or do a late night feeding," the woman next to Emmie riots.

Macy raises her hand and I'm half-afraid of what's about to fly out of her mouth. With my sister, it's pretty much a crapshoot. We'll either get kicked out on our ear or the whole room will love her.

"You have to be pro-active," she says in that know-it-all sarcastic way that oddly seems to draw people in. "There are a lot of singles' activities this month that are totally acceptable to attend. I just went to that blind date with stupid Cupid thing out in Cider Cove."

A small groan evicts from me.

Great.

Either she's trying to push this investigation into overdrive or she's genuinely trying to give the girl some questionable advice.

Madeline opens her mouth to speak and someone shouts from the back, "I heard a murder took place out there."

"See that?" someone shouts. "Looking for love is *dangerous*."

Another woman belts out a laugh. "Who needs men when we can have good friends and *wine!*" She lifts her glass and everyone does the same at the inadvertent toast.

The glorified sommeliers come around and quickly refill our glasses. Shockingly, both Emmie and Macy are on their third, and we've hardly started painting the ocean.

I glance over at Madeline, and she takes a breath as if she needed a moment to collect herself. I'm sure she doesn't hold those smart-aleck remarks—bordering on rude—against these women.

Sure, they're bringing up the murder, but how were they supposed to know she knew the deceased?

But Macy knew for a fact that Madeline was at the inn the night Lad was killed. Leave it to my spicy sister to cut right to the investigative quick. Macy operates best in a contained environment, not where the liquor flows freely, thus inspiring her mouth to do the same.

The hour plods on, and soon enough we're wrapping it up. Women stretch their limbs while walking around admiring one another's work. There's a line to the restroom six women deep, and both Macy and Em are still imbibing as if we had stumbled upon the fountain of youth—more like the fountain of booze.

Madeline makes her rounds, nodding in approval at all the Caribbean blue beachscapes she comes upon in replicate. She heads our way and a part of me wants to muzzle Macy, but it's too late. Madeline is already upon us.

"Great work." She winces at Emmie's canvas, which looks decent if you were looking at the world from Salvador Dalí's perspective.

She steps my way and tips her head to the side, but she's not looking at my artwork. She's looking at me.

"You know, you look very familiar to me, but I can't seem to place you. I'm embarrassed to say it's been bugging me for the last half hour. Did we go to high school together?"

I step over to her while Emmie and Macy do their best to drain every bottle in this joint.

"We might have met." I give a guilty shrug. "Emily Carter invited my friends and me to check out her art centers, and, of course, we decided on the sip and paint." I nod over to Emmie and Macy as if to prove my point. "I'm the manager at the Country Cottage Inn. Were you at the blind date with Cupid shindig? I met so many people that night it's hard to keep track." Liar liar, paintbrush on fire, and probably my face and underwear, too. I hate to lie. Not to mention I'm terrible at it.

She sucks in a quick breath and slaps her knee. "Yes! That's where I remember you from." Her expression changes on a dime and she's morbidly somber. "That was a terrible night. Lad was my friend." *And so much more.* "He was...the best." *I wanted to say he was everything to me, but there's no use in admitting it now.* "I just can't believe he's gone." Her eyes flood with tears. "But I plan on keeping his memory alive." She blinks rapidly. "He was a very big part of the Carter Art Centers. He was the meat and potatoes of it if you ask me. Emily ran her art centers like a business, but when Lad stepped in, he treated every employee as if they were family." ***Of course, I would be less of a sister and more of a wife.*** A private smile twitches on her lips.

Oh wow. Madeline was having an affair with him, wasn't she?

I clear my throat. "It sounds like he was quite a guy. Had he been with the company for a while?"

"Not long enough. I've only known him for about a year. He and Emily were sort of a quick burn—more like a flash fire." ***Something you'd want to put out and forget about.*** She shakes her head as she gazes out at the wall. "I can't believe she's alive and *he's* dead."

"Excuse me?" I blink back, trying to digest what that might mean.

Her fingers fly to her lips before they melt their way back down to her side. ***Did I say that out loud? Oh heck.***

"I'm embarrassed to admit this, and I hope you won't think less of me, but she was, you know, old enough to be his mother. I'm not used to that."

"I know what you mean. My own mother, who has at least a couple of years on Emily, dated someone my age—my own boyfriend's brother." I got over it pretty quickly, but for the sake of milking this visit for what it's worth, I'll play along.

"No!" she gasps with delight and I think I fully have her trust now. And I didn't mind throwing my mother under the cougar bus one bit to get it. "How did you handle it?"

"It's over now. But it was odd while it lasted for so many reasons." True as God. "Anyway, I can understand where you're coming from. So Lad and Emily were the real deal, huh? I just met her briefly that night. That's when she extended the invite to check this place out. They looked like a solid couple from what I could tell. He seemed really devoted to her."

Madeline takes a breath. "I don't know about that. I mean, I guess he was. There wasn't a hint of a sign that he was going to leave her." *No matter how hard I pressed.* "But he was never affectionate with her in public." *Not the way he was with me in private.* "I mean, if I had a boyfriend, I'd want a little handholding, a public peck once in a while, but there was nothing. It's almost as if it was a business arrangement. Or maybe he was showing her some sort of respect. Not that I wanted to see them making out in front of me." She glances to the ceiling. "But, I mean, they were engaged. Most engaged couples that I know act as if they're in love."

Wow, Georgie is right. This world is full of ageist elitists. Not that I can point a finger after that Mom and

Maximus catastrophe. And actually, they were pretty good together.

"How close were they to tying the knot?"

"This spring." She nods. "Oh, and Emily's daughter was not very happy about it. I'm shocked the sheriff's department hasn't arrested her yet. She threatened to kill Lad on numerous occasions. Of course, it was said in jest—*angry* jest, but no one thought she'd actually pull the trigger—pardon the gun pun."

"When was she threatening him? Did a lot of people hear this?"

"The whole company. We have a meeting twice a month and Paige would wait until Emily and Lad would leave before she started badmouthing him. She made it clear she wasn't a fan. I'm sure she's dancing a jig right now." Her features harden. ***She's the easy suspect. Everyone knows that. I'll have to point the sheriff's department in her direction. Maybe there's a tipline? It's about time Paige gets what's coming to her. Threaten to fire me, did you? I'll get the last laugh yet.***

A loud bang erupts from our right and it's Emmie who's knocked down her palette, only to leave a nice colorful blotch on the floor.

"Oh no!" I head over, trying to remove the palette from the floor, but it's suctioned itself to the vinyl, and the more I try to lift it, the bigger the rainbow acrylic blob I create.

"Don't worry." Madeline whistles and a group of the former sommeliers morph into the cleanup crew. "You girls go ahead and take your paintings. We'll get the rest of this. It was nice seeing you again." She leans in. "I'm sorry, but your name escapes me."

"Bizzy. Bizzy Baker."

"That's right!" She snaps her fingers before she shoots me with them. "I do remember that." *I remember thinking Busy Body. But she seems nice enough. And it felt good sharing those things about Lad. I miss him. I miss his beautiful face. Those strong arms. I'd give anything to have him back. But then, it was his time to go. I don't think it could have worked any other way.*

She says a quick goodbye and ducks into a space behind a floral curtain in the back.

That was odd.

She looked pretty emotional, but I can't get over her cryptic words—not to mention her far more cryptic thoughts.

Madeline was having an affair with Lad Warner.

And what did she mean by "it was his time to go"?

Lad was in his prime. He was seemingly healthy.

Perhaps if I saw her drinking tonight I could have excused her bizarre inner dialogue, but she didn't have a sip from what I could tell.

No. Something is very, very off about her. I just don't know what.

I do my best to collect Emmie and Macy as I schlep all three of our canvases while herding us back out into the street.

"Hello, Edison!" Macy shouts at the top of her lungs into the darkened sky and a few cars give a honk of approval. Or disapproval. Take your pick. I'll go with the positive vibe for now.

Emmie jumps up onto a stack of trash bags set out front as if she were climbing a mountain.

"Hey, Edison!" Emmie shouts. "I hear you're the bad boy of New England!"

"Here we go," I mutter to myself as I give Em a yank and she practically falls into my arms, sending all three canvases in my arms sprawling over the sidewalk.

"*Bizzy,*" Macy shrieks at the top of her lungs and some nebulous being shouts for us to keep it down. "You're ruining my art!"

"Your art is fine," I say, collecting the slightly smeared canvases that loosely qualify as art as she put it. "Let's get in the car."

"I don't want to get in the car," Macy bellows with all her might as if I were standing on the moon.

Macy and Emmie sing a few verses of our favorite country song—out of tune, but admittedly it doesn't sound so bad—and I'm half-tempted to join them.

And in a fit of solidarity to sweeter days gone by, I toss my inhibitions to the wind, albeit without the aid of a good glass of vino, and I belt out a few verses with them. Just as we're getting to the chorus, the whoop of a siren goes off and stuns us into submission.

To my horror a sheriff's cruiser pulls up alongside us and out steps Deputy Leo Granger looking more than amused as he recognizes us.

"What do you want?" Macy exaggerates every word like only the belligerent can.

"I'm here to see the show." He sheds his signature wicked grin. Leo always looks as if he's in on some deep, dark secret, and in my case, he most certainly is.

Macy looks at Emmie. "You hear that? He's here to see the show, girls. I say let's give it to him!"

Emmie belts out a riotous laugh. "One—*three!*"

On *three*, both Emmie and Macy lift their sweaters, right along with their over-the-shoulder boulder holders, and within seconds Leo Granger informs us he has four very perky reasons to arrest us all for indecent exposure and disorderly conduct among a litany of other things.

In fact, he does just that.

And being the kind gentleman he is, he gives us a ride all the way to the Seaview Sheriff's Department in the back of his cruiser.

It looks as if I'll get to see Jasper tonight after all. That is, if he feels like visiting me in my holding cell.

Note to self: Macy and Emmie are no longer a part of my investigation squad.

6

The sheriff's department is located in the heart of downtown Seaview, and even this industrialized business district looks far more welcoming than anything Edison has to offer. A plethora of pink and red hearts hangs from every window and door. Love is in the air, all right, even right here at the sheriff's department. Which seems fitting, considering the fact the love of my life works here.

It took both Leo and me to help Macy and Emmie stagger their way into the monochromatic world before us and into the suspect processing center. The floors, the furniture, and the counter all share the same white with navy stripe. There's a handful of deputies mingling about, looking official with papers in hand.

A few ornery looking men and women stand behind the counter before us and I can't help but note they look as if they'd rather spend their evening getting a root canal. Which is an idea I could totally get onboard with. I'd rather see Jasper at work as a visitor than an incarcerated member of dysfunctional society.

"I can't believe you landed us here," I say as I jab Macy in the ribs with my finger.

"*Ow!*" She pulls Emmie forward like a human shield. "I don't even *knows whys* we're *heres!*" Her voice hikes to stratospherical levels.

"The fact you can't piece together an intelligible sentence should be your first clue." I turn to find Leo speaking to someone behind the desk. "*Leo,*" I hiss his name like a reprimand. "You and I both know I don't belong here, and neither do they. I could have easily thrown them into the back of my own paddy wagon and had them in Cider Cove by now."

He tips his head back, examining me with pursed lips. "Now what fun would that have been? Don't worry, Biz. Jasper's still on the premises." He turns and nods to someone across the way. "Camila, I need Jasper. Bizzy's been detained."

"Ugh." Why does it genuinely feel as if I'm socked in the stomach each time I hear her name? "Leo, we both know she won't help in that department. If she had her way, she'd lock me up and throw away the key. Now give me back my purse and I'll call him myself."

Leo confiscated our things as soon as he threw us into the back of his patrol car—something about making sure we didn't have any contraband.

"Can't," he says it flat. "I haven't searched it for weapons yet."

"Good Lord, you are going to get an earful and a fistful, and maybe the working end of a baseball bat the next time you try to enter the inn."

A dark laugh erupts from him as he holds up his hands.

"All right, all right." He sheds a wide grin. "I'll get Jasper myself."

No sooner does he leave than Camila shows up with that wicked smile smeared across her face like the smudge of sarcasm it is. Her dark hair is pulled into a high ponytail and her lips are a ruby shade of red that would look garish on me, but, as fate and good genetics would have it, looks amazing on her. She's donned a low-cut red sweater, a tight pencil skirt that forces her to walk like a mermaid, and pin thin *sky-high* heels. She looks much more suited for Fashion Week in New York, or a hot date, than she does to pull a nine-to-five behind the desk at the sheriff's department. It's not until I get a closer look at her nametag that I gasp.

"Homicide division secretary?" I choke on the salty choice of words begging to stream from my lips. "Boy, you work fast."

"That I do." She gives the brass plate on her chest a quick tap. "I always get what I want, Bizzy. Don't forget that."

Emmie belches like a frat boy as she falls over Macy for support, and Camila wastes no time in laughing at the two of them.

"Oh, what a show." She holds out her hands and claps their way and they take a rather unceremonious bow that has them stumbling to a nearby bench. "How about you, Bizzy? Did you flash your chest at Deputy Granger, too? I heard there was public nudity involved when he called it in over the airwaves."

"Nope, I bared my fangs, sort of the way I'm doing right now. I don't belong here and neither do they."

She clucks her tongue. "If I had a dime for every time I heard someone in the processing center say those words. Don't worry. I'll make sure Jasper's not lonely while you're doing time in the big house. "

"Please, as if he would ever want to spend time with you."

Before she can offer up a rebuttal, my tall, dark, and vexingly handsome boyfriend appears with an eyebrow hiked.

"Bizzy?" **When Leo said he had a surprise, this is not what I envisioned.**

"*Jasper.*" I leap over and wrap myself around his warm, strong body. The woodsy scent of his cologne alone makes me feel safe—and somewhat anxious to pull him into the nearest corner and have my way with him.

A small bark emits from his side, and I look to find Sherlock Bones making himself known.

Bizzy? Did you stop by to rescue me? Did you bring bacon? His old girl beast is here. And she's threatened to chop my tail off if I keep wagging it!

He tucks it between his legs as if he were still fearful Camila might be wielding a pair of scissors as he speaks.

"Sherlock," I say and bend over and kiss his sweet face. "Nobody is chopping off your tail," I whisper before straightening.

Camila leans toward Jasper. "Thank you for lunch. It was wonderful. It's nice to know you still like spending time with me." Her dark eyes cut my way. **I guess there is still someone who doesn't mind spending time with me, and he just happens to be your boyfriend. For now.**

My lips part as I look up at him.

He shakes his head as she makes her way back to her hidey-hole, which unfortunately for me is right next to *his* hidey-hole.

I wonder if Jasper would be up for a career change anytime soon? Although it's no use. She'll just do what she does best: stalk him into oblivion.

"I'll explain later." He grimaces my way. *It looks bad. But hopefully once I let her know it was a bear trap I fell into, she'll understand. A bear trap that I will never fall into again.*

"No need to explain. I trust you." *And I can read your mind*, I want to add.

I shrug as if it were no big deal, and in a way it isn't.

Leo quickly gives him the rundown on why we're here.

"You went to a bar in Edison?" Jasper gives me the side eye as if he were trying to put the real pieces together per our earlier conversation. "Wait a minute." He ticks his head back. "Leo, this bar wouldn't happen to be on Union Street, would it?"

Leo nods. "That would be it."

Macy raises her blonde mop. "*Theys* got strip clubs, too!"

"Good Lord." I shake my head at Jasper. "*Wes* didn't go to a strip club."

A smile curls into the corner of his lips. "I know. You went to the Carter Art Center, didn't you?"

"Boy, you really are a good detective." I bite down over my lip flirtatiously. "Go easy on me, Officer. I'm a first-time offender."

"Leo"—he turns to look his way—"why don't you go ahead and drive Macy and Emmie back home? Help them get settled. I've got a suspect interrogation I need to get to concerning the Warner case."

"Ooh, can I come?" A thrill tingles from my head to my toes at the prospect.

"Of course." Jasper wraps his arm around me. "That suspect would be you."

"You're not funny," I say as I give his tie a quick tug.

"How about dinner?" There's an unforgiveable twinkle in his silver eyes that every last part of me has grown to appreciate.

"Dragon Express?" I tip my head at the mention of our old standby. Jasper and I enjoy takeout from there at least three times a week.

"I was thinking about something a bit more formal. You know, for processing purposes."

"Sounds good, Detective. Maybe we can swing by Edison to pick up my car?"

"Then that's the plan."

I leave Macy and Emmie in Leo's capable, albeit wily, hands as Jasper, Sherlock, and I head out into the frozen February night.

I'm ready for romance—and a little physical interrogation from the sexiest homicide detective in all of New England.

Once we pick my car up, we take Sherlock back to my cottage to spend some time with Fish and Cinnamon. I already have Georgie popping in for the evening to feed and let them out. She mentioned she was going to teach them poker, and I let her know that was on her.

After I freshen up a bit, Jasper drives us out to what he refers to as a "secret location". It turns out, that secret location is in Whaler's Warf. And as soon as we park, he leads us to a snazzy seafood restaurant called the Blue Crab Seafood Grill.

Jasper and I enter the dimly lit establishment and are seated next to the window where we can see the boats docked in the harbor just a stone's throw away. On the table sits a heart-shaped votive candle and there's a tiny cutout of Cupid adhered to the window next to us, signifying that indeed it is the most romantic time of the year.

We each opt for the special, and as the waitress takes off to fill our orders, Jasper reaches across the table and takes up my hand.

"Bizzy"—there's an apologetic sternness in his eyes—"I have to ask again, this time for the record. What happened that night? Tell me the exact timeline of events as you remember them."

"The night of the singles mingle." I nod. "I went into the ballroom and I was talking to Georgie and Elvis Hendrix—he's the organizer—when Emily and Lad came along. Georgie thought Emily was Lad's mother and it was really embarrassing, but that was quickly cleared up. They're engaged, or at least they were. Anyway, Emily really seemed to like him."

His chest bounces with a laugh. "I should hope so. She was about to marry the guy."

"Well, I'll get back to that in a minute, and you won't believe what I have to say about it." He sheds an amused smile before I continue. "Then he spots some guy in a suit, by the door, and makes the comment that this suit guy, Colt, has poor timing." I leave out the part about that being just a thought. "So he takes off and Emily notices her hemline is a few inches longer than the rest of the women's in the room and she takes off to hike up her skirt. But before she can get too far, her daughter, Paige, intercepts her. Which is a good thing because Paige was looking for them when she arrived." I lean in. "Actually, she was looking for Lad, and she specifically said she could kill him, which according to Madeline is something she says a lot. Anyway, I'll get to that, too. And then—"

"Whoa, *whoa*." He signals for a time-out with his hands. "You are by far the cutest amateur sleuth I've ever met in my life."

"Hey? Who are you calling an amateur, buddy?"

Jasper belts out a laugh and there's a twinkle in his gray eyes that fills me with warmth.

"I'm sorry," he whispers through a pained smile. *What I wouldn't do to make this beautiful woman my wife.*

A breath hitches in my throat.

"*Jasper,*" I whisper without meaning to.

"What is it?"

"Oh." I startle back to reality. "I, um, didn't get to tell you about Madeline. She ran into me while I was holding Cinnamon. That's Lad's labradoodle. She's the one that taught the art class I took Macy and Emmie to tonight. It was a sip and paint, and sort of an all-around disaster as you witnessed. Anyway, back to the night of the killing. Madeline was seen running from the front doors of the inn. And after the murder—"

He nods. "Madeline was in the ballroom. I know. I spoke with her briefly that evening. I got the feeling she very much had strong feelings for Lad."

"Try an affair."

He tips his head. "She told you that?"

"Not in so many words. Oh, and there was a redhead that night—"

"Natalie Weiland." He twists his lips. "Runs a bookstore in Seaview."

"Ooh, a bookstore," I coo. "Colt told me she was with Lad at some point—as in romantically involved."

"Really? It sounds like Lad got around."

"He certainly had a past. But that's not the strangest part." I lean in. "I talked to Emily after the murder and she expressed she was putting on a show, that she would have to wait until she got home to express her rage."

Jasper leans back a notch. "Let me guess. She said that in not so many words?"

An exasperated sigh expels from me. "Yes."

"Bizzy, how are you surmising these things? Are you some kind of expert in reading body language?"

"Only yours." I give a sly wink. I read their minds. Which brings me to my next point. This is the perfect opportunity to tell him. I give a quick glance around at the other patrons. Okay, so it's not exactly ideal. I should probably do this back at my place, and seeing that Jasper is at my place just about every other night when I'm not at his place that shouldn't be a problem. Although, in my defense, we find far more interesting ways of entertaining ourselves. And filling him in on my supernatural status is never at the top of the list.

"Hey." He pulls my hand forward and gives it a kiss. "I'm sorry. I didn't mean to insult you. I'm in love with you, Bizzy. You mean everything to me. And yes, you are intuitive. But I'm afraid..." There's an edge to his voice as he says it. "I'm afraid you're going to find yourself in a very dangerous situation if you keep this up—one that I won't be able to help you out of."

"I promise"—I lean forward as far as the table will allow—"I didn't and I won't put myself in a dangerous situation. There were at least a hundred women at that sip and paint tonight. Okay, so that's a slight exaggeration. More like fifty. I wasn't alone with Madeline. And, if I happen to stumble upon another suspect, I'll make sure I'm not alone with them either."

"Bizzy, I couldn't live with myself if I gave you the go-ahead to be in the same vicinity with another suspect. Why are you so bent on pursuing this?"

"Because *I'm* a suspect."

Jasper's jaw redefines itself. "Did you kill Lad Warner that night at the inn?"

"*No*." It streams from me with a marked exasperation, and a few people at a nearby table pause to turn this way.

"Then I formally clear you from the suspect list." A devilish grin glides up his cheek. "You have no reason to pursue this case any longer. Let me do my job, Bizzy. I'm good at it. I promise I will catch this killer."

The food arrives before I can offer up a formal rebuttal.

Jasper and I indulge in a surf and turf meal to end all meals on land or sea and we don't hesitate to hit the dessert as well.

Jasper taps my finger. "What was it that you were going to tell me?"

"Oh"—I wince over at bodies filling up the establishment—"it can wait."

His glowing eyes search my features and I can genuinely feel his affection for me.

If she says it can wait, it can wait. As far as I'm concerned, we've got a lifetime. And soon enough, I'm hoping she'll agree.

My gaze locks over his.

Jasper is thinking about taking our relationship to the next level. That means I owe him answers to questions he doesn't even know to ask.

It looks as if time is running out. I need to do this. I want to.

I'll make sure it's the first order of business in the next few days—right after I talk to Paige Carter.

Madeline might be trying to set her up for Lad's murder because she tried to get her fired, but those thoughts Paige had the night of the murder were suspicious in and of themselves—thinking if only she could fake feeling sick, she might be home free?

Free from what?

Logic would dictate murder.

7

February carries a chill in the air, frosty enough to hold the promise of another ice age. And the brisk winds only seem to be picking up today. Jordy is outside of the inn, trimming the bushes, and I'm about to step out to speak with him about a complaint of a leak when Georgie bustles in through the doors, and by her side is a dark-haired fiend with a mischievous gleam in his eyes.

"Elvis Hendrix." I drum up a half-hearted smile. "Welcome back to the Country Cottage Inn. Hello, Georgie. What are the two of you up to this afternoon?"

Fish jumps down from the counter and wraps herself around my ankles until I scoop her up into my arms.

Is this the killer, Bizzy?

I shrug down at her.

Sherlock and Cinnamon lift their heads our way with half-closed eyes before deciding to continue with their naps.

Georgie's wiry mane is windblown and her purple and gold kaftan sits askew as she struggles to straighten it.

She nods my way. "Elvis wanted to take another look at the ballroom if that's all right with you. His next shindig is already trending on the Dependable app. All of his users are excited to see how he's going to top that murderous blind date with Cupid." She leans in. "Only, they're calling it a blind date with the Grim Reaper."

"Wow, okay. Sure," I say, looking up at the older man dressed in a tie-dyed T-shirt with a thermal on underneath to keep from catching pneumonia. "If you need any help with decorating or catering, of course, the inn will be happy to oblige."

Elvis cranes his neck in the direction of the ballroom. "I'm actually looking to see if the energy levels are optimal for amorous connections. There was quite a negative force field here that night. And if it hasn't vacated the building, then I'm afraid I'll have to find somewhere else to host the event."

Georgie links arms with him and pulls him close. "Don't you worry, big boy. I've got my sage and a lighter. We'll have all that negative juju up in smoke in no time."

"And the inn along with it. No to the sage," I'm quick to protest.

Fish yowls as she jumps from my arms. *Sherlock, Cinnamon! Georgie is about to burn the building down!* She runs their way in a panic.

"Elvis?" I take a step closer to him. "What do you think happened to Lad that night? It was a pretty violent end."

He takes in a breath as he shakes his head. "I wish I had an answer. Lad was a good guy."

Georgie gives his arm a tug. "Even good guys have enemies. Who hated the guy enough to pull the trigger? You didn't do it, did you?" She looks my way and winks. *I'll prove to you yet, I'm not dating a killer.*

Elvis bucks with a laugh. "It wasn't me. I can assure you of that. You of all people should know I'm a lover, not a fighter."

A deranged smile glides over Georgie's face. "I can affirm that, Bizzy. Many, many times."

So much for *not* dating a killer.

Don't judge me, Bizzy. Georgie narrows her eyes over mine. *I have a weakness for men in power. Who could resist the king?*

Duly noted.

Elvis rocks back in his Birkenstock sandals—*socks* with sandals, might I add.

"You know"—he squints out at the ceiling—"that daughter of Emily's, she never made her dislike for the guy a secret. But pulling the trigger seems a little over the top." His mouth widens a moment as if a thought were coming to him. "You know, there was a relative of his, a man who had a sinister energy."

"Colt?" A tiny burst of excitement rockets through me at the thought of being a step ahead in the name game.

He snaps his fingers. "That's the guy. Whenever he came around, Lad would walk him over to the corner and they would have a private little chat. Always tense. I had to leave the room. I couldn't stand the—"

"Negative energy?" Georgie gives his ribs a quick tickle.

He nips at her lips with his giant maw as if he were about to swallow her whole.

Elvis blows her a kiss. "I love it when you finish my sentences for me, Gray."

Gray?

I make wild eyes at Georgie for accepting the murky moniker.

"We'll see you later, Bizzy." She hustles the king of hearts over toward the ballroom and I spot a giant bouquet of sage emerging from her tote bag and a lighter.

Good grief. She really is about to burn the whole place down.

I'm about to head that way when I spot a redhead out by the fountain.

Is that Natalie Weiland?

I head on out into the icy air and I do a little quick step over to Jordy out by the bushes.

"Jordy—two things: There's a leak in room eighteen, and Georgie is about to burn the ballroom down."

"Geez, Bizzy." He puts his shears down and flips up his goggles. "A leak *and* a fire? You wouldn't happen to have a body you'd like to throw into the mix, would you?" he says it playfully with a wink.

"Watch it, Jordy. It just might be yours."

He takes off and I head over to the redhead by the fountain just as she's rising from placing some flowers at the foot of it, in the exact spot where I found Lad Warner lying on his back.

She turns to leave and startles at the sight of me. "Oh, you scared me."

"Sorry. I can see you were having a private moment. I'm Bizzy. We met that night. You run the bookstore in Seaview, right?"

"I do." Her eyes widen a moment. "Lad was an old friend. I just felt I needed to say goodbye. If you want, I can take the flowers away."

"No, please leave them. I completely understand. It's fine, I promise. And I'm sorry for your loss."

She sniffs into the wadded tissue in her hand. Her red hair is cut to her shoulders, her face looks pasty and puffy, and her mascara is trailing down her cheeks in muddy tears.

"He was a good man. We spent a lot of time together." She shrugs. "Dated off and on. But then, who didn't Lad date?" A tiny laugh bumps through her and her eyes brighten as if she needed just that.

"I'm sure that makes it harder. You knew him a little more intimately than the rest of us."

"That's for sure. I'd like to think I knew everything about him, but people can surprise you. His engagement to Emily was certainly a surprise. I guess they were in love."

"I heard not everyone was in support of their relationship. Someone mentioned Emily's daughter had it out for him." A couple of someones.

She blinks my way as if she were surprised I knew.

"Oh, she did," she's quick to affirm it. "Between you and me, I think all that anger came from the fact she wanted Lad for herself."

"What?" I gasp at the thought. "But her mother—"

"Isn't a very nice person. I heard Lad was showing some interest in Paige first right up until Emily decided she wanted him for *herself.*"

I hold my breath a moment to digest this. Lad was into Paige *first*?

"And he chose Emily over Paige," I say. "Interesting."

She shakes her head. "Not so interesting when you consider which Carter woman has more money." Her eyes scour my features for a moment. *If only she knew how true that was.* "It was nice seeing you again, Bizzy." She starts to take off, and I don't feel settled where we left off.

"Natalie? Your bookstore—you wouldn't happen to have a section on relationships, would you? I'm currently building up the nerve to tell my boyfriend something about my past."

"Yes, we have a fabulous self-help section. I'm over at the Water's Edge Bookshop. Stop by anytime. I know all about relationship troubles. I'll be happy to help you find just the right book."

I know all about relationship troubles. Heck, I could write a book.

Now could she.

Maybe while I'm grilling Paige, I'll ask her a few questions about Natalie, too.

I bet she'll have a few interesting things to say—about a lot of things.

8

After hanging out in the café and noshing on one too many raspberry cheesecake bites, I decide to deep dive into my investigation of Paige Carter.

"Where is she, Bizzy?" Georgie asks as she cuddles with Cinnamon. She has Sherlock at her feet, rapt at attention as he watches her dip in and out of her pocket to produce bits of bacon one pinch at a time. Georgie is famous for harboring cured meats in her kaftan.

"I don't know." I blow a stray hair out of my eyes. "But I do know she works with the company. Maybe she runs one of the art centers?"

Emmie comes over and leans against the counter with me.

"I don't care how much free wine they'll try to lure me out there with"—Emmie shudders as she says it—"I'm not going."

"Good." I bump my hip to hers. "Because you're not invited."

"Who's not invited, where?" a deep voice strums from behind, and I spin to find Leo Granger standing there in a red and black buffalo flannel and a pair of worn-out jeans, a far cry from his deputy's uniform.

Emmie grunts at the sight of him. "You are definitely not invited."

A smile slithers up his face and—is he flirting with her?

My mouth fall opens. "What's going on, Leo? You look dressed to thrill." *And it won't be my best friend you're thrilling.* "Looking for Mayor Woods?" *Thrill her. Lord knows she could use something to wipe the scowl from her face.*

His brows tweak. "I just had breakfast with Mayor Woods this morning at the Breakfast Bender."

The Breakfast Bender is a place right up the road on Main Street where they serve pancakes the size of your head.

"Hear that?" Georgie whacks me on the arm. "He's cheating on you, Biz."

I'm quick to shake my head. "It sounds to me, Leo was doing me a favor."

Leo belts out a laugh. "You're welcome." He sobers up. "So where are you off to? This has something to do with an investigation, doesn't it?"

Emmie chortles. "He's got your number, Bizzy." She takes off for the register to help a group of customers who just wandered in.

Georgie butts her shoulder to mine. "So where are we off to?"

I look right at Leo. "I want to ask Paige Carter a few questions. Just need to find her first." I pull out my phone and type in her name along with Carter Art Centers and, sure enough, the entire screen is quickly populated.

"Found her." Leo nods to his own phone. "She's teaching a class." He shoots a wry smile my way. "What do you know? I'd say chances are good there will be wine."

I click into the same descriptor. "It's a sculpting class. It starts in less than an hour and a half. It's all the way in Rose Glen." I glance at the time. "I think I can make it."

Georgie gives Cinnamon a squeeze. "I think *we* can make it."

Oh no. Cinnamon is quick to protest. *I'd much rather spend the afternoon lounging with Fish. Count me out, Bizzy. But I'll be happy to discuss the case with you. I miss talking shop with Lad.*

He may not have been able to communicate with me as you can, but he sure carried on a lively conversation in my presence as if he could.

Leo and I exchange a glance because I'm certain he heard the exchange as well.

"Okay, Cinnamon. You can stay with Fish. But you'll have to be in the Cottage while I'm away. And as soon as we can, I'd like to dig into those conversations you had with Lad. You never know. Anything might help."

Sure thing. As long as the killer is arrested. It boils my blood to think someone out there is happy that my Lad is gone. And happy they've gotten away with it so far.

"It boils my blood, too," I say as I scoop Cinnamon into my arms and gift her a kiss on the top of her furry little head. "And that's exactly why I'm going to hunt down the killer."

Rose Glen is a quiet, scenic town just a twenty-minute drive from Cider Cove. The Carter Art Center is set in the heart of its rather polished downtown district, sitting on a hill pushed against a dense forest of evergreens.

The building itself is a series of sharp squares with floor-to-ceiling windows that feature giant floating canvases, and every one of them features scenes from the local landscape. The entire state of Maine is an artist's dream with its dramatic rocky crags, sheer cliffs, white sandy beaches, forests and mountain backroads, not to mention lakes, rivers, and the grand Atlantic that stretches out like a sheet of heavenly blue right into the horizon.

No sooner do Georgie and I get out of the car than a red truck pulls up that I happen to be more than familiar with.

"Good Lord," I say as I link arms with Georgie as if I were about to float away.

"It's Leo," she hisses. "I think he's onto us, Bizzy."

"Of course, he's onto us. We shared our whole strategy with him over raspberry cheesecake bites."

"Something tells me he wants to find the killer first, and he's riding on your coattails to do it."

Leo laughs as he strides our way. "You got me there, Georgie." He folds his arms across his chest as he looks to me. "I'm sorry, Bizzy. Either you need to rethink heading inside or I need to go in with you."

"For your own peace of mind?" I'm almost amused by his presence. Almost. Mostly I'm annoyed.

"For Jasper's. You and I both know he wouldn't approve."

Georgie scoffs. "You men and your controlling attitudes. Nobody tells my Bizzy where she can and can't go. Just because you have a pseudo-limb swinging between your legs doesn't mean it gives you the right to dictate what women can or can't do."

Leo inches his head back a notch. "Nobody is trying to control either of you." It comes out sweet, tender even. "But Jasper and I work for the law. And as stewards of public safety, we can't in good conscience send you off into potential danger. Either of you."

Georgie tosses a hand in the air. "He's got us there, Bizzy. There's only one thing left to do."

"I agree," I say.

Leo's left brow arches with curiosity. "Packing it in and heading home?"

A dull laugh brews in my chest. "We're inviting you to join us. For our protection, of course. Georgie is thinking about expanding into sculpting, and I'm here to support her."

"Yeah." Georgie jabs a feisty finger in his direction. ***Bizzy, you do realize I hate working with clay.***

Leo gargles a dark laugh. "You do realize I can read minds." A wicked grin expands across his face.

"Drats." Georgie snaps her fingers in a fit of frustration. "Well, come on, hot stuff. We've got a killer to catch."

The three of us head on into the light and airy building with its impossibly high ceiling. We quickly fill out the paperwork and pay the fee to join the sculpting class and head back to the studio where we find Paige helping students get settled into their spaces.

A couple of long tables stretch across the room, and there's a giant glob of clay as big as my head staked over the workspace in front of each student.

Paige quickly calls for us to each find a free workspace before doing a double take in my direction.

Her blonde hair is pulled back into a pert little ponytail and her face is dusted with powder, right down to her eyelashes giving her a soft look. She's donned her signature bright pink lipstick and, I'll admit, it's a shade I wish I could pull off with ease. When I venture into the deep end of that hue, I look like a crazed teenager who just ravaged a bag of cotton candy. Suffice it to say, it's not a good look on me. Not a sane look, either.

She doesn't hesitate striding on over. "I recognize you." Her affect brightens. "From the inn, right?"

"Oh, that's right." My voice hikes a notch and I take a tiny bit of pride in how natural my surprise sounded. "Your family owns these centers, isn't that right?"

She gives a quick nod. "My mother." ***Thank God Lad no longer has his clutches into her. That was a close one.*** "I help run classes. And, of course, the business will be mine once my mother retires. I'm learning every angle I can. Right down to teaching." She gives a warm laugh. "I'm an artist at heart, so it's no stretch."

"Perfect," I say. "My friend Georgie works in mosaics, but she's thinking of branching out."

Georgie steps forward, a gleeful smile budding on her lips.

"Your mother invited me to try out the studios anytime. And here I am. I brought friends, too." She gives a cheeky wink. "Say, you wouldn't be looking for a mosaics teacher, would you? I've got a gig doing a city beautification project along Main Street, but that good time won't last forever, if you know what I mean. We artists have to stick together."

The woman's eyes bulge for a moment. "Maybe. I guess when you're done with the city project, come by and I'll see if we can work the class in. I think that might actually be fun."

Georgie gives a wild clap and a cheer. "Woo-hoo!" she bellows so loud, the entire class turns at attention. "You're looking at a future professor here, kids." She jabs her elbow toward the class before looking my way. "I'll go get the three of us a seat. I can't wait to get my hands dirty."

Thank God I brought Georgie. She couldn't have added more authenticity to this outing if she tried. And who knows? She might have scored a job out of the deal.

Leo hitches his head toward Georgie. "I'd better make sure she doesn't break anything. Or knife someone." He says that last tidbit under his breath before heading to the rear where Georgie has already wrangled the attention of half the class.

"She's a bit of a character," I whisper to Paige. "But she's one of my favorite characters."

Paige bubbles with a laugh. "Don't worry. I love her already. That's the thing about the art world. You meet the best people. I certainly don't miss corporate America."

"Oh? What did you do before this?"

"Inventory for a shipping company down in Seaview. Believe me, it was as tedious as it sounds. But once my mother started dating Lad, I thought I'd better head over and keep an eye on things."

"Really? What things?"

She makes a face. "The guy was five years younger than me. And don't get me wrong. I have nothing against May-December romances, but as soon as he put the moves on my mother, I thought something was up."

My heart thumps wildly. This information is almost as good as an admission of guilt.

I lean in. "Were you right?"

"I think so. Look, I know it doesn't paint a good picture of me. But Lad was a handsome man. My mother, she's—a woman who doesn't like to go out, doesn't care to hike, or do any of the things Lad liked to do. He basically came in and swept her off her feet. I'm sorry. But I suspected he was a gold digger right from the start." *And boy was I ever right.* She stares off blankly while shaking her head.

"I bet your suspicions were confirmed."

She looks up and nods. "My mom had a prenuptial agreement worked out, and there was only one contingency to him signing."

My lips part as I wait with bated breath. "What was it?"

"He wanted half of all of her assets, liquid and real estate, should she pass away."

"Oh." I give a few quick blinks. "Would that be so unreasonable?" I wince because I immediately regret the words as they sail from my mouth.

"Yes, trust me. If it were your mother, it would be entirely unreasonable. My mom and dad built an empire in the art world. And as their only living heir, it steamed me that this—*stranger* whom she had only known a few months would have an equal footing to my inheritance. I thought it was insane."

"Did Lad ever sign the agreement?" It's an easier question than asking if Emily actually agreed to give him half of everything.

"Nope." She folds her arms across her chest as she shudders. "He was rubbed out before that ever happened. They were all set to go last Tuesday, only Lad never saw last Tuesday."

Well, there's a motive for murder if ever there was one.

And *rubbed out*? That's a killer's catchphrase.

"How's your mother taking all this?"

She closes her eyes a moment. "Hard, I guess." **Not his death, but what she gleaned right before it. But I can't open that can of worms right now. I promised her I wouldn't tell a soul. She's right. It's humiliating to the core.**

She shakes her head my way. "Class should be starting now."

"Oh right." Humiliating? Exactly what did Emily glean? "Paige?" I ask, scooting in a notch before my opportunity quickly dissolves. "Did Lad have any enemies that you know about?" *Other than yourself*, I wanted to add. I have a feeling I won't have to look too much further for Lad's killer. Either Paige did it herself or she hired a pro to *rub* him out. But would a pro really leave their weapon at the scene of the crime?

She straightens as she glances to the back of the class at the circus surrounding Georgie.

"You know"—she ticks her head to the side—"I didn't really know Lad all that well. He has an old girlfriend though, Natalie Weiland. I think she would know him better as far as who did or didn't like him. But he was a strange character. He had eccentric taste. He conned my mother into buying really odd pieces, acrylics, and oil paintings that go beyond the pale of modern art. They weren't anything special if you ask me. They weren't even from an established artist. Well, I guess they were, but I had never heard of the guy. Anyway, if you want to entertain yourself, you'll have to see the paintings for yourself. Next Tuesday at two. That's when the meeting gets out. I'll be there. The acrylic offenses are hanging in the corporate boardroom. My mother paid a mint for them." She shakes her head. "And I'm pretty sure they're worthless."

She calls the class to order and I make my way to the back, taking a seat right between Georgie and Leo while Paige gives us instructions on how to sculpt a human head.

She encourages us to feel our neighbor's face with our eyes closed, and just as I'm about to team up with Georgie, she quickly gloms onto an older gentleman sitting next to her in a T-shirt with a picture of a bowtie and suit jacket. I can't help but make a face at what a perfect pairing they are. Georgie somehow always manages to winnow out a prize for herself when we're on the hunt for a killer. Not that Formal Tux T-Shirt Guy is a prize, but you have to give Georgie props for trying.

I spin in my seat until I'm facing Leo Granger.

"Don't get any funny ideas," I say. "I can read your mind."

Leo and I close our eyes and begin mapping out each other's faces with our hands.

So I'm going to do it, I say. *I'm telling Jasper the truth. Have you thought about what I asked? Are you up for doing it yourself? You never know, it might restore your friendship.*

Leo sighs and I can feel his cheeks flexing into a frown.

"I don't know, Bizzy," he whispers. *You tell Jasper your truth. I'm still trying to figure this out. In a way I think it will be a shock all on its own for him to know what you're capable of. If you throw me into the mix, he might feel left out in an odd way. I don't want to hamper anything the two of you have any more than I might have already.*

"That's fair," I say. "And nice. But if you don't tell him, then there's still one more secret I'm holding from him."

Leo pulls back and we sit and stare at one another for a good long while.

"Okay, Bizzy. I'll do it for you and for Jasper. But only because I'm rooting for you guys. Just give me a heads-up when you tell him."

"Will do," I say. He turns to start in on his sculpture, and I lay my hand over his until his dark eyes are trained on mine once again. "Thank you, Leo. This means a lot to me."

We get straight to sculpting, and once the hour is through Leo and I each have what resembles an alien being on our hands.

Georgie's project looks like the second coming of Michelangelo.

"Georgie, that's fantastic," I gasp in awe as I take in the bust of a beautiful woman with a slightly familiar mischievous gleam in her clay eyes. "Who is that supposed to be?"

"That's me about thirty years ago." She carves a flower in her wavy hair, and then I see it—Georgie's features, her crooked smile. "I miss that kid." She gives her look-alike a playful slap.

The three of us donate our projects right back to the art center clay pile and I thank Paige for class as we're leaving.

"And I might pop in and see that artwork in the corporate office," I say as we head for the door. "I was telling Georgie about it and she's fascinated."

Paige gives a quick nod. "I'd encourage you to buy it all off me, but I'd hate for you to have to mortgage your house," she teases. "Take care." She gives a cheery wave before tending to another student.

Mortgage my house? Exactly how much did Lad have Emily spend on those paintings?

We head out into the icy February air, and I'm about to pluck the keys out of my purse as I stop cold at the sight before me.

Leaning against my car with a hardened stare aimed right for Leo is Jasper Wilder.

"Bizzy, Georgie." He gives a slight nod, but he never takes his angry stare off Leo. "Granger." He stalks over and pulls Leo in by the shirt before giving him a violent push. "How dare you." *I'd kill him, but there's one too many witnesses.* "Don't feed me this 'I'm not into Bizzy' bull. We both know you've got some sick vendetta against me and you're pulling out all the stops."

Leo's chest pumps with a dry laugh. "Which is it, Jasper? Am I into your girl, or am I out to get you?"

Jasper growls, "Maybe it's a little of both."

Leo shoots me a look. "Let me know when *it* goes down. I can't wait to prove him wrong." He jumps into his truck and speeds off.

Georgie rummages through my purse before coming up victorious with the keys to my car.

"Ah-ha!" She rattles them in the air before jumping into the driver's seat and rolling down the window. "Hey, Detective!" she shouts over at Jasper. "Get a clue. This woman right here is going to need a ride home." She wags her crooked finger my way. "If you want to kiss and make up, there's a great B&B just up the road. Ask for the red room of shame. You won't regret it!" She speeds off with a screech to the tires and I groan as I look back at Jasper.

"How much do you dislike me right about now?" I cower a little as I look his way.

"Zero." A sly grin glides up his cheeks as he pulls me in. "How about a quick bite?"

"Out of me? In the red room of shame?" I bat my lashes up at him as I tease him mercilessly.

A laugh rumbles from him. "I think I can wrangle out a lunch break." He softens a notch and there's a look of regret in his eyes. "I'm sorry I was hard on Leo. I couldn't help myself."

"I won't hold it against you. I'd much rather hold myself against you. Are you up for coffee? I hear Rose Glen has a bakery down the street that makes a mean red velvet cupcake."

He gives a slow nod. "And then I'd liked to take you out to a bookstore in Seaview if you have time. I hear they have a great section on how to find a killer."

My mouth falls open. "Are you inviting me into your investigation?"

His brows hike a notch. "If you can't beat 'em, join 'em." *I'd much rather Bizzy go out with me than Leo.*

I give a simple nod. "It's a date."

My lips close over his, and Jasper and I share a heart-stopping kiss right here in the parking lot of the art center.

Soon he'll know everything there is to know about me.

And I sincerely hope it's not the beginning of the end.

9

Jasper and I hit the We Need Dough Bake Shop hard as we buy up enough sweet treats to feed the entire inn. And we get it all to go, along with two hot lattes.

We decided to nosh in his truck on the way to Seaview, and while we're on the road, I tell him all about the strange art Paige told me about that hangs in the corporate office, and the fact Lad died days before Emily was going to agree to give him half of everything.

He shakes his head as he swallows down the rest of his red velvet cupcake.

He ticks his head my way. "And what about the dog?"

"Cinnamon?" I perk up at the thought of that curly-haired cutie. "What about her?"

"Don't you think it's strange that Emily hasn't claimed her?"

"Not really. Emily was in a miserable state that night. She may not be a dog person. And I don't think Paige was close to Lad or his dog. She made it clear when I spoke to her there was no love lost between them."

"All of that is strange. And it moves Paige up the suspect list. I get it, she was trying to protect her mother. She really made the guy sound like a sleaze."

"I think he was. I mean, Paige didn't have to work too hard to make him look like a gold digger. What do we know about his past?"

"Not much. He graduated from a nearby university with a degree in agriculture."

"Agriculture?" I ask as if I didn't hear him right.

"Yup. That's about all I know."

"What about his employment history?"

"That's the thing. I couldn't find any."

"Wow. The guy was in his late twenties. You would think he would have held down a job by now."

"You would think." He shrugs. "And I'm sure he did. Off the books, I'm betting."

"You're probably right. I can't wait to talk to Emily. I bet she'll be a wealth of information. I mean, did she know anything about his past at all?"

"I don't know, but when I do talk to Emily, I plan on meeting her at the corporate offices. I'm thinking I should bring Ella."

"Ella?" That's Jasper's sister. She works at an art center herself. "That would be perfect. While you casually interrogate Emily, she could pepper the conversation with genuine questions that pertain to art."

"Exactly." He nods out the window. "And I'm hoping Natalie Weiland will fill us in on a missing link to this puzzle." He casts those gray eyes my way for a moment and it feels as if a spotlight just centered over me. "I was about to head down to talk to her one more time, right after I spoke with Paige."

"And you wisely invited me." I shed a greedy grin. "Trust me. It's a good thing. I'm a woman. Women connect to other women better. It's a proven fact. Besides, I've already connected with her. We talked about books a bit." Self-help books that could assist me in divulging a deep, dark secret to the love of my life. A thought comes to me. "In fact, why don't we split up once we head inside? That way I can get some one-on-one time with her. There's no telling what she might divulge once I get her going."

His lips purse as he considers it. "All right. But I'll be watching you. Try to stay out in the open. Make it easy on me. And treat the questions with kid gloves." *If the department knew I was depending on a civilian to run an interrogation, I'd have to turn in my badge and my gun before the day was through. But this is Bizzy. She can run circles around any of those deputies down at the station. Not that I'd tell her. I'd hate to encourage her and send her running into harm's way because of it.* "But just this once, Bizzy. Because we're doing this together."

"You bet." I feed him a frosted brownie and he moans through the bite.

Something tells me she knows exactly what to do to get anything she wants out of me. And I do not object. I'd give her anything. Give up anything for her. Let's hope my career doesn't fall into that category.

The Water's Edge Bookshop sits exactly where its name suggests, on a stretch of real estate right along the coast.

It's a quaint little shop with a stone façade and a row of weeping willows planted out front. A giant wisteria shrub arcs over the entry with its lavender flowers still budding to perfection, giving the place a cozy appeal. Inside, the sweet scent of paperbacks livens the air with its homey perfume, and I'm instantly transported to the libraries and bookstores of my youth.

"Jasper"—I pull him in close—"is there anything more intoxicating than the scent of old books?"

"I can think of a thing or two." A devilish grin crests his lips.

"Ha ha, and thank you, I think." My teeth graze over my bottom lip. "But seriously, I really need to get a bona fide library going at the inn. There's a small lending library in the grand room, but I'd love to have wall-to-wall bookshelves filled with delicious smelling paperbacks and hardbacks for the guests to read at their leisure. And me, of course. I'm a bit of a bookworm myself."

"I'll make a note of that." *A bouquet of roses and a bouquet of books for Valentine's Day.*

"Now you're talking." I give a little laugh. "You're a man after my own heart. By the way, a bouquet of books is ingenuous."

He inches back and glances from side to side. "Did I say that out loud?" *I must be losing my mind. I'd swear I was thinking it.* "I'm pretty sure I'm going crazy."

"Oh!" My fingers fly to my lips. "No, you whispered it." Lovely. Make the poor guy think he's losing his mind. This isn't going to end well. This secret of mine needs to come out, and fast. "Anyway." I spot a redhead over by the back wall, shuffling through a few boxes of inventory. "I see Natalie." I point her way. "Get lost, would you?" I give a little wink before dotting his lips with a kiss. "And don't worry. You're my favorite kind of crazy."

I take off and pick up a few books on my way over in that general direction.

"Natalie?" I clear my throat as she stands to her feet and turns around.

Her pale face brightens once she sees me. "Bizzy! You came." Her red hair is knotted over her head and stray wisps fly about her cheeks like flames.

"Yup." I glance over my shoulder and I'm pleased to see there's no sign of Jasper. Not that I plan on keeping him a secret. "I'm actually here with my boyfriend."

She gasps as she slinks my way. "The one you're keeping the secret from?"

I give a quick nod. Natalie is one person I'm thrilled to pull deeper into my rabbit hole. The more she trusts me, the more she'll be willing to tell me. I hope.

She gives a scrutinizing glance around but comes up empty.

"Well, let's get you to the self-help section and we can winnow away the books and see which one is the best fit for you. It's right over here."

We walk a few aisles over and I can just about feel Jasper getting edgy. For some reason, his thoughts are muted, most likely because I'm so focused on Natalie at the moment.

She's donned a red wool vest over a white turtleneck and her vest has a series of pink heart-shaped appliques that run down the front. The bookstore is decorated with cutouts of red hearts set against white doilies and metallic cutouts of Cupid as well. The décor de jour this time of year.

"I can't believe it's almost Valentine's Day," I muse as she peruses the titles.

"Tell me about it. I used to love that holiday when I had an official boyfriend. But you're still in the running for fun."

"It would be fun, but I think that's the night I'm going to spill my big secret."

Her mouth falls open as she gives me her full attention.

"Really?" Creases form around her eyes as she looks me over. "Are you sure about that? I mean, people usually go out on Valentine's Day with certain expectations." She says that last part with a husky growl. "Is it the kind of secret that could end up ruining the rest of your night?" She leans in, looking genuinely concerned for the precarious state of my libido. And rightly so.

I shake my head. "I don't know. It's the kind of thing that can go either way. It's basically a weird quirk of mine that I'm hoping he'll accept."

She waves me off. "Is that all? You'll have no trouble. And if he doesn't accept you for who you are, he wasn't worth it to begin with."

"I suppose you're right." Only, I have a feeling my telesensual status will prove to be the exception. "So how about you? No prospects to celebrate the upcoming big day?"

Her eyes glaze over as she stares off at the books before us.

"Nope. Things sort of ended badly with my ex."

"Can I ask what happened?"

"Oh, Bizzy." A dull laugh pumps from her. "You would not believe me."

"Try me." I shrug. "In fact, it might be good for me to hear something unbelievable that happens to be true. At least then I'll know how my boyfriend will feel when I spill the big news."

She tips her head to the side. "You got me there. All right. But strictly for experimental purposes. This is to help you, not me. I'm a lost cause."

We share a warm laugh.

"I don't believe that," I say.

I really do like Natalie. And oddly enough, I'm starting to consider her a true friend.

"Okay"—she sags for a moment—"he left me for someone he had nothing in common with." She shrugs. "Granted, I eventually met his new plus one and she was nice and funny and cute in a *grandmother-ish* sort of way. The worst part? He seemed genuinely happy. Anyway, we reconnected as of late and he was coming back to my place and we were having dinner and laughing. I thought there was a chance we were going to reconnect romantically as well." *Lad loved me. And I loved Lad. The thought of everything we had going up in smoke—in gun smoke. He was inches from coming back to me, and now he's gone forever.*

My mouth falls open as I examine her.

"Natalie, I'm so sorry." I shake my head as genuine tears come to my eyes. "When I saw you by the fountain at the inn, you mentioned you and Lad dated. Natalie, this ex-boyfriend you're talking about, it was Lad, wasn't it?"

She takes a breath and closes her eyes before a tiny nod shudders from her. Her shoulders hike up a notch just as she breaks down in deep, convulsive sobs, and I don't hesitate pulling her into a strong embrace.

"Oh, Natalie. I'm so very sorry for your loss," I whisper as tears of my own streak my face.

She pulls back, quickly wiping down her tears.

"Thank you." She shrugs. "It's been really hard. It's not like I can openly grieve him other than as a friend. And everyone is giving Emily their condolences, as they should. But I feel the pain, too. What I wouldn't give to have him back." She sighs hard before pulling out a tissue and blowing her nose.

"Who do you think would do something like this to Lad? I mean, it did happen at the inn, which I manage. I keep asking the sheriff's department, but they're clueless as to who could have done it and why."

Her eyes widen as she shrugs. "It could have been random. I really don't know. I've been thinking about it, though. I saw Lad and Emily arguing out by the fountain as I was headed out to put my coat in the car. And then I went back into the ballroom and not long after, rumors started to swirl about a murder. Whatever she was angry about, she was angry enough to kill."

Something Paige said internally comes back to me. She mentioned Emily had gleaned something from Lad right before he was killed, something that humiliated her to the core.

I blink over at Natalie. "So Emily was upset."

"Very." She leans in. "And Lad told me not too long ago that she carries a gun." Her eyes well up with tears again.

"Did you tell the sheriff's department?"

"I can't remember anything I said to anyone that night. I hardly remembered you. Sorry. I was a bit shaken."

"No, that's okay." I know for a fact she hasn't spoken to Jasper again after that night. "I can let them know. I've been cooperating with the sheriff's department. They've come by every day since." *The lead homicide detective just so happens to live at the inn*, but I leave that residential tidbit out.

Her lips cinch. "There's one other person they should probably look into. A man by the name of Colt Ferguson. He and Lad had some crooked dealings." She shudders. "I always told Lad that Colt was trouble."

"What kind of trouble?"

She glances over my shoulder. "The guy deals in crooked loans."

"Like a loan shark?"

She gives a single nod.

"Why would Lad need a loan—a dicey one no less? I mean, Emily is loaded. She could have easily lent him the money."

"That was bound to happen." She gives a husky laugh again. "But it didn't. Before Lad met Emily, his grandfather's farm fell on hard times and he wanted to help him out." She shrugs. "He needed money fast and he took a loan out."

"That's what people do, I guess." I shrug back, trying to minimize my concern.

The chime on the door goes off and she glances that way.

"I'd better see if they need help out front. I hope you find your book, Bizzy."

I glance to the endless rows of self-help books and I'm pretty sure not one of them covers the supernatural topic I'm in need of.

"Actually, after talking to you, I feel better about the whole thing."

"Good." She clasps her hand over her chest. "I'm so glad. I just know he'll accept whatever quirk you're about to lay on him. Men are much simpler creatures than we give them credit for." Her eyes cloud over with darkness. "Sometimes I wonder if we're the ones that complicate things."

God knows I'd still be with Lad if things weren't so damn complicated.

She starts to take off and a thought comes to me.

"Natalie? The inn is hosting another event thrown by Elvis Hendrix, the maker of the Dependable app. It's this Saturday night. I'm sure you already know about it. I mean, since you're a member of Dependable."

"Right." She shakes her head. "But I hadn't heard of it, though. Thanks for the heads-up. I don't think—"

"I won't take no for an answer. You came to the blind date with Cupid looking for love." Even if it was a desperate attempt to get Lad back, which I'm starting to believe it was. "Who knows? Maybe this time you'll find it. For real." Those last words come out soft and tempered, and I really do mean them.

She nods. "I'll think about it."

She takes off and I spot Jasper by the mystery section, so I head on over.

"Find any clues?" I tease as I touch the spine of an Agatha Christie novel.

A naughty grin glides up his cheek. "I'm betting not as many as you."

We hightail it out of there and jump into his truck before speeding out of the lot.

I quickly relay the entire conversation, sans any mention of the secret that I plan on divulging at some point soon. Natalie really did offer up some sound advice. I'd like to think Jasper could overlook just about anything.

"A farm, huh? That makes sense. But if his grandfather is a farmer in need of money, I'm sure he would have qualified for loans on his own."

"Maybe he didn't want to take a loan out? Maybe he was too prideful for that?"

"Maybe. But typically farmers aren't a prideful bunch."

"What about the murder weapon? Natalie said Emily carries a gun. Lad told her himself."

Jasper tips his head to the side, his mouth opening and closing.

"Why do I sense a reluctance in the force?" I ask, knowing full well why he's hesitating. "Let me guess. It's classified information?"

He sucks in a breath through a grimace. And then, just like that, Jasper lets out a deep sigh.

He nods toward the road. "I'm not sure if Emily owned the gun. The weapon you found was traced back to a pawn shop in Edison. It was sold to the killer about a month ago."

"A month ago?" I bounce in my seat. "That might as well have been yesterday. Who was it registered to? I bet that will lead straight to whoever did this."

"Maine doesn't require a firearm to be registered."

"*What*? Why not? It seems like common sense."

"I agree, but that's the way it works right now. Which means—"

"Which means we have no way to know who fired that gun."

"Not yet."

"Not yet," I echo. "What about forensics? What did they find?"

His lips twitch with a smile. ***Forensics. It's as if she's talking dirty to me.***

"They found two sets of prints. Yours and mine—and, yes, we have yours on file."

"Wonderful."

Someone fired that gun and it wasn't me.

Someone brought a weapon to my inn, killed a man in cold blood, and left me holding the smoking gun—and I very much plan on getting to the bottom of it.

10

The Booze and Babble?

I stare up at the banner erected outside of the ballroom with a mild sense of disbelief. Bodies mill about as Elvis Hendrix's latest catastrophe in the making gets underway.

"So that's the best he could come up with, huh?" I say to Nessa as we watch the masses stream into the ballroom from underneath an arch of pink heart-shaped balloons.

"I guess." She shrugs as her red dress glitters under the lights. "It was a last-minute endeavor, so I guess we need to cut the guy some slack. Hey, you don't think we're going to find another dead body tonight, do you?"

"Nope," I say it with a touch too much confidence, when really I should have none. But then again, Nessa is my employee, and I want her to feel safe within her work environment. Speaking of safe. "Besides, Jasper has arranged for half the Seaview Sheriff's Department to have a presence at the inn. You couldn't be safer if you were on the moon."

Fish jumps in front of me, and I quickly scoop her into my arms.

I don't feel safe, Bizzy. And neither should you.

"Aww." Nessa gives Fish a quick stroke over her back. "The poor thing looks frightened out of her mind. It's almost as if she knows."

"She knows plenty," I say as I dip a quick kiss between Fish's eyes. "Sorry, girl. I'll hold you tight." I hitch my head toward the ballroom. "Grady is manning the fort, and I say it's time to party, Ness. Who knows? There might be a heart-shaped surprise in store for you, too."

She gives a little skip. "Now that puts a spring in my step."

The ballroom is festooned from floor to ceiling with balloons, streamers, and paper pompoms in every color of pink and fuchsia. It's a virtual wonderland of doily-laced romance, and the room is twice as packed as it was that fated night.

Elvis has essentially transformed the ballroom into a wine tasting venue. The only thing he requested the Country Cottage Café provide was Emmie's raspberry cheesecake bites. And seeing that nearly everyone is holding one in their hand, right along with their wine glasses, I'd say they were a pretty big hit.

The sound of soothing love songs filters through the speakers. And even though just about everybody is swaying to the music, there aren't any couples officially dancing at the moment. Nessa takes off for the tables brimming with booze, featuring wine in just about every color.

A giant glittery sign is erected at the front of the room that reads *don't risk your romantic future to just anyone, trust us—we're Dependable!*

"Bizzy Bizzy," a familiar deep voice calls from behind and I turn to find my father with his arm linked to a gorgeous brunette with a tight-lipped smile—Jasper's mother, Gwyneth.

"Dad!" I offer my dapper daddy a quick hug before offering Gwyneth a quick embrace as well. "Gwyneth, you look amazing," I say, taking in her long black dress. The old me would have made a mental quip regarding a coven, but Gwyneth and I have moved beyond our rocky past. I hope. I think. I *pray*.

Fish slaps me on the nose with her tail. ***Hold me tight, Biz. Word on the street is, she's looking for a familiar.***

"You're funny," I whisper.

"Bizzy." Her expression sours as she gives my hair a quick flick. "You must see my hairdresser. She takes on even the most desperate of cases."

Dad lifts a finger. "And on that note, I think we'll speed ahead to the wine tasting portion of the evening."

"Good call," I say.

They start to take off and Dad hops back on one leg.

He winks my way. "Once I get a little liquor in her, she tends to loosen right up."

They dash away just as I spot my sister shuffling her way over. She's donned a frilly pink number that has her looking like a saccharin confection. That coupled with the sour look on her face makes for a delicious candy-coated irony.

"Don't you say a word." She points right at me. "And give me my furry little niece."

Macy scoops Fish out of my arms. "You, my little princess, are about to be my wing cat."

"Wing cat?" I'm not sure if I should be amused or frightened.

"Yeah, you know. They say pets and babies are chick magnets. Well, it works the other way, too. This place is crawling with detectives and deputies and the sheriff himself. I'm taking a page out of my baby sister's playbook—the chapter on snagging yourself a man of the law." She leans in. "What's not to love about a man who brings handcuffs along on a date?"

"Stay away from the wine," I advise as she strides off, much to Fish's furry protest.

I'm about to make a run for the raspberry cheesecake bites when a redhead pops up, dazzling the room in a sleek silver gown that looks as if it were a disco ball in its previous sassy and, might I add, sexy life.

"Wow," I say as I jump back. "Natalie, you look fantastic. You don't play fair, do you? All the other women in the room might as well go home."

She tosses her glossy red hair back and belts out a laugh.

"You're too kind, Bizzy. I feel like a human reflective strip. I like *your* dress." She gives a nod to the navy number I've donned. It's an A-line linen sheath that touches above my knees with a layer of chiffon over it to soften it. This isn't the first time I've pulled it out of the closet, but it's the first time Jasper will see me in it.

"Believe me, I'm not the one stealing the show. You look like you're ready to take on the world. And I'm really glad you came. I think this is a step in the right direction. You have a life to live."

She takes a breath as she glances around. ***And Lad doesn't.***

"I know I should feel terrible being here." She shakes her head. "Being anywhere, but I guess it would be nice to get out there again and meet someone." *Someone who actually knows what it means to keep their word.*

I tip my head to the side. What could she mean by that?

She nods to the refreshment table. "I'd better get a glass of wine in me before I turn around and leave the room." She takes off, and no sooner does she take up a glass than the bartender strikes up a friendly chat with her.

That didn't take long. Good for her. She deserves a little attention tonight, and many nights thereafter.

Speaking of attention, I scan the room for Jasper, and instead, I find Georgie and the king himself as they speed this way.

"You both look fabulous," I say, marveling at the fact not only is Georgie wearing a purple kaftan with pink sparkly hearts stamped over it, but somehow, in some alternate universe, Elvis is wearing a shirt that looks strikingly similar.

Elvis twirls in his glittery getup. "Georgie dared me to wear it, and I'm not one that backs away from a dare."

Georgie pulls him close. "It was a Valentine's Day special. Buy one get one for your man. It tells the world we're a power couple."

"You're a couple, all right," I say, trying my hardest to read his mind.

Yup. I'll do anything for fifty bucks. Ten minutes and I'm ditching the duds and maybe the psychedelic princess now that I see a silver beam of light calling my name.

I follow his gaze to Natalie and my mouth falls open.

"Do you know Natalie Weiland?" I ask, practically calling him out on it.

"Is that Nat?" His expression quickly sours. "Yeah, I know her. That was Lad's chick. The first one." *That's no silver beam of light. More like a portal of darkness. That's all right. There are plenty of short skirts where that one came from. And I plan on catching a few before I leave.*

Figures. Elvis developed Dependable as a means to an end—his own end, in his own bed.

"Elvis"—I choose to ignore his perverted mental musings for a moment—"why do you think she and Lad broke up?"

His eyes widen a moment. "Let's just say Lad had a hankering for the finer things in life. And Natalie, well, she just works in a bookstore."

Georgie groans, "Sounds like he was looking for a sugar mama."

Elvis shakes his head. "You said it, not me." He nods my way. "I don't like to speak ill of the dead."

"How did the two of you meet?" I ask him. "You and Lad?"

Elvis squints into the crowd. "Sports bar. The guy put the fan in *fanatic* for just about every sport you can think of. Word got out that I was working on Dependable and he wanted in on it. Lad always wanted in on the ground floor. He liked to turn a buck."

Georgie smacks him on the stomach with a wink. "Who doesn't?"

A pair of warm arms wraps themselves around me from behind, and judging by that heady, thick, spiced cologne I know exactly who it is.

"Whoever you are, I think I'm going to kiss you before my boyfriend gets here. I'm a bit lonely." I spin on my heels, landing a kiss over his lips and Jasper hums a dark laugh.

"You think we'll get caught?" he whispers right over my mouth, and I bubble with a laugh.

"With you? It's a risk I'm willing to take. But you might want to watch your back. He's packing heat."

Jasper looks to Georgie and Elvis.

"Sorry I'm late, but it was for a good cause. Georgie, I have great news for you. I spoke with Juniper Moonbeam's attorney, and I know exactly what she's doing time for."

"*What?*" Georgie and I sing like a choir.

"Bribery charges." He nods to Georgie. "Apparently, she had racked up quite the stack of traffic tickets. And once she figured out there was a warrant out for her arrest, she tried to bribe a city official to have them removed. And that garnered her exactly twenty-two days in the Collingsworth Correctional Facility."

Elvis groans, "I'm sorry, Georgie. I didn't know your kid was in prison."

Georgie shoots him a look. "Don't knock it till you try it. She's playing doubles on a tennis team, and they serve rice pudding with cinnamon for dessert."

"Georgie"—I shake my head at my sweet friend—"I can promise you, she doesn't want to be there for long."

"And she won't be." Jasper lifts his chin. "She's being released Monday. I told her attorney to expect a call from you."

"Monday?" Georgie gives a wild clap. "I need to go. I need to get all of my ducks in a row and make sure Juniper Moonbeam lands in Cider Cove safe and sound. Your father said he'd help." She pulls me in and kisses my cheek. "Thank you, Bizzy." She pulls Jasper in and kisses him on the lips. "Thanks, hot stuff." She looks to Elvis and waves him off. "You go chase those skirts. I don't need to be a mind reader to know where your head is."

He opens his mouth as if to refute the idea before his lips stretch across his smarmy face. "Thanks, Georgie."

The two of them disappear into the crowd, and I look over at Jasper, only to find his lids dangerously hooded.

He leans my way. "Can I have this dance?" It comes out like a rumble of thunder, and every last part of me wholeheartedly approves.

A laugh gets caught in my throat as I give a quick look around and moan.

"Oh shoot." I make a face. "No one is dancing yet."

"Then I say we start a trend." Jasper wraps his arms around me and glides us to the middle of the room, and slowly but surely other couples follow suit. Jasper holds me close and the heat emanating off the two of us could start an inferno.

Soon, it seems the entire room is swaying to the rhythm. It's safe to say Jasper and I started a trend.

Jasper dots a kiss to the top of my head. *I love this woman, and I want everything with her—for life.*

I glance up at him as my heart riots in my chest.

Jasper wants everything with me.

And I bet that includes the truth.

The event winds down, and I help to make sure the cleanup gets underway. I spot Jasper saying goodnight to his mother, and I'm about to head over when I cross paths with Elvis.

"Thank you, Bizzy, for the do-over. No one died, so I'm counting it a success."

"Indeed." I'm about to take off when I lift a finger. "Elvis, did you and Lad have any mutual friends?" *By the name of Colt, maybe?* But I don't ask that. I'd like to see if he comes up with a broader pool of people who couldn't stand Lad that I may not have come across yet.

He clucks his tongue. "No, but we shared a bookie."

He takes off and my mouth falls open.

They shared a bookie?

I have a feeling Lad Warner had a hard time keeping his hands on a dollar bill.

That's exactly why he'd need a dicey loan.

And that just might be why he needed a sugar mama, too.

Now to do a little digging to see if I'm right.

11

"We should definitely have a crudité platter," Emmie says while working on her Valentine's Day craft project.

It's Monday afternoon, and I've yet to find evidence to solidify the fact Lad Warner had a gambling problem.

I spent the morning checking out old guests and checking in new guests, and there's finally a lull at the reception desk so I can get back to my research.

"Vegetables?" I glance up at Emmie. We've been tossing menu ideas for the Valentine's Day dance back and forth. Mayor Woods hired the Country Cottage Café to bring refreshments, simple appetizers, and desserts to the community center. To quote Mack, *Lots and lots of those raspberry cheesecake thingies. They make me tingle.*

Neither Emmie nor I was sure what to make of that.

I wave a cheesecake bite at Emmie, and we both break out into laughter.

"Try not to tingle," she says, picking one up herself.

"It's hard not to. These taste so good, I'm surprised Mackenzie hasn't outlawed them yet."

"Something tells me she won't outlaw vegetables." Emmie shrugs. "We need to have a variety and veggies aren't complicated."

"Crudité it is."

Sherlock lifts his head from the floor, his eyes still heavy with sleep. *Don't forget the meat tray, Bizzy. And make sure to leave one platter behind on the counter at the café.*

I tip my head at him curiously.

Sherlock moans. *Georgie says you have to toss meat that's been left out on the counter overnight. And I say, feel free to toss it my way.*

Fish yowls, *Always thinking,* while furiously licking her paw.

Cinnamon lets out a sharp bark. *I like how he thinks. I'll help him eat it, Bizzy. Leave twice as much out on the counter overnight. My mouth is salivating already.*

I nod her way before looking to Emmie. "We'll need a few charcuterie boards as well—a variety of cold cuts and cheeses—maybe a little bacon to round things out."

"Consider it done," she chirps.

Fish jumps up onto the marble counter, watching attentively as Emmie fills four large glass tubes with candy conversation hearts. She plans on putting a small votive candle at the top of each vase once they're full. It's going to look adorable, even if it does have the potential to melt hearts literally.

"Emmie, where do you get these bursts of brilliance?" I ask, leaning in to inspect one of the works of candy-based art before her.

"Where I get all my bursts of brilliance. Pinterest."

A laugh thumps through me as I get back to my laptop. "If only I can get a burst of brilliance and figure out who killed Lad Warner in cold blood right here at the inn."

Cinnamon lets out a few sorrowful moans and Emmie quickly scoops up the curly-haired cutie.

"Don't you worry." Emmie kisses Cinnamon on the top of her auburn head. "Nobody is going to hurt you," she says in her best baby voice. "In fact, I'm going to make sure you're safe and sound."

I suck in a quick breath. "Emmie! Are you thinking about adopting Cinnamon?"

Cinnamon lets out a happy yelp, and Emmie laughs as she dots the pooch's face with another kiss.

"Only if no one comes up to claim her. Obviously, the poor girl's family is in shock. They might come looking to collect her after the funeral, or who knows when."

"Emmie, that's so nice of you." I reach over and give Cinnamon a scratch over the back. "Hear that? You might have just found yourself a brand new mama."

Fish yowls. *That means we'll be neighbors. Emmie lives a hop, skip, and approximately three scampers up the road.*

Sherlock lifts his head again, slow and lumbering as if it weighed a thousand pounds. In all fairness, it is his naptime. He vocalizes something shy of a bark. *I'm glad you're not leaving, kid. Georgie keeps a pocket full of bacon at all times. She's our supplier. And according to my nose, she should be here in less than five minutes.*

My fingers dance over my keyboard. "I just can't find anything on Lad Warner that leads anywhere. I give up."

"You're not allowed to give up, Bizzy Baker." Emmie dumps another bag of conversation hearts into a tall glass vase. "Try looking up a suspect."

"That's a good idea. I need to track down Colt Ferguson. Natalie said he dealt in crooked loans—as in a loan shark. I bet he knows all about Lad's gambling problem." I input his name, and to my surprise the entire screen is populated.

"Would you look at this? I finally hit pay dirt. I think I need to listen to my bestie more often."

"I agree." She leans over and gives a quick glance to the screen.

Fish jumps into my lap and gurgles. *Don't keep us in suspense, Bizzy. What do you see?*

Cinnamon gives a soft bark. *Is it Lad's killer?*

"I don't know if he's the killer. But it looks as if Colt Ferguson is a part owner of a seafood restaurant out in Edison called Marty's Got Crabs."

"*Ohh*!" Georgie comes barreling this way with a bright red kaftan flowing behind her like a kite. "Marty's Got Crabs is the perfect snazzy place to meet my Juniper Moonbeam. She's on a bus as we speak. She's getting dropped off at Bar Harbor and then taking a cab to a secluded spot where the feds won't find her."

Both Cinnamon and Sherlock spring up at attention.

Our queen is here! Sherlock spins in a circle and moans right at her. *Georgie is here, and she's rich with bacon!*

Cinnamon lets out a quick bark. *Don't forget me. For goodness' sake, I can't exactly jump to the floor.* She whimpers up at Emmie with those big brown eyes. *You'll have to feed me.*

Emmie flicks her fingers at Georgie without hesitation. "Hand over the bacon, woman."

And Georgie does just that before tossing a few strips to Sherlock as well.

I shake my head at her. "Georgie, why would the feds care where your daughter is headed? Jasper said she was released."

She waves me off. "You can't trust those guys, Bizzy. Once they've set their sights on you, they've got a bead on you for life." She pulls out her phone and starts tapping away. Less than a second later, her phone pings. "Juni is meeting us at Marty's Got Crabs at six o'clock."

Emmie gives a little hop. "I am so going."

"I'm going for sure," I say as I look down at the screen at a picture of Colt with his hand wrapped around a man who looks as if he could be his brother. I bet that's Marty. And I bet Colt put up the funds to finance the place.

Now if only I could prove all of my suspicions, especially the ones I have about Lad.

Georgie scoops Cinnamon right out of Emmie's arms.

"My baby is coming home! My baby is coming home!" She dances an odd little jig, wiggling and giggling in places that leads me to believe one could inadvertently weaponize select body parts. Georgie's chest springs around the room as if she were throwing yoyos and both Emmie and I duck for cover. "Oh, you girls." She waves us off. "So what if I don't wear an upper decker flopper stopper? One day you'll wake up and draw a line in the chest basket sand." She makes a dash for the door. "I've got to get dolled up if I'm going to get me some crabs. I'll see you out front in a couple of hours!"

Emmie waggles her brows. "Georgie seems to think this place is snazzy. If I'm lucky, the place will be crawling with single hot guys—none of which will have crabs themselves."

"Georgie thinks a taco night at the local commune qualifies as a debutante ball. I'm pretty sure the single women of Maine should steer clear of any establishment that boasts of having crabs. All single women who enter those questionable, most likely STD riddled doors should abandon all hope of finding good honest men whose crotches don't double as petri dishes for fun new diseases. Promise me I won't find you in some corner making out with a man named Marty."

"Fine." She picks up Fish and now they're both glaring at me. "This is purely a reconnaissance mission."

Sherlock gives a little bark. *Bizzy, you promised Jasper you'd let him know if you were even thinking about speaking to a suspect.*

I twist my lips over at the freckled pup and nod.

So I did.

I pull out my phone and text Jasper to see if he's up for dinner tonight. No sooner do I hit send than those dancing ellipses appear on my screen.

Sorry. I'm on a secret mission. But if you don't mind, I'd love to stop by and steal a kiss or two or twelve.

I text right back. **Make it a baker's dozen and we've got a lip-locking deal.**

Jasper is on a secret mission. I'm not sure what it means for him, but I certainly know what it means for me. I'm heading to Edison. And if I'm lucky, Colt Ferguson will be there, too.

12

Marty's Got Crabs is more or less what you'd expect it to be. The building itself takes up quite a bit of raunchy Edison real estate. There's a towering neon sign with a picture of a fisherman clad in a yellow slicker, and over his crotch sits a shiny red crab. Surprisingly, this doesn't seem to deter the masses who are busy streaming their way into the establishment.

"Look at that crowd, Bizzy." Emmie butts her arm against mine. "We'll be lucky if there's not a two-hour wait."

"We can sit at the bar," I say, cinching my coat tight around me. It's freezing out, and I'm thankful I'm still dressed in my jeans and a sweater underneath my winter coat. "Most places will still serve the full menu even if you're bellying up with a vodka tonic."

"Sounds good." Emmie gives a frenetic nod, which turns into a full-blown chatter of the teeth. She's opted to wear a little black dress and heels, along with a tiny pink faux fur coat. It's clear Emmie decided not to heed my warning about abandoning all hope, and instead, it looks as if she's made peace with the fact a fisherman with a crustacean hanging off his blue jeans might be the one for her.

Georgie links arms with me. "Let's get in there, girls, before our tatas freeze and fall right off our bodies." She hustles us inside where the air is warm and holds the scent of French fries and cheese biscuits—two scents that I just so happen to wholeheartedly approve of.

There's a crowd in the foyer and the waiting area is packed, so I nod for Emmie and Georgie to follow me to the bar where it's dimly lit, the music is upbeat and a touch too loud, and a group of men are having a salty conversation at a table in the corner.

"The entire left side of the bar is empty," I say. "Let's get a move on, ladies."

"Save a seat for Juni!" George swats me with the enormous tote bag she's got strapped over her shoulder with a picture of a cat on the front, and I can't help but note the fact it feels as if she struck me with something solid.

"What the heck do you have in there, Georgie?" I say, giving the bag a poke as we take up four barstools on the end. "A human head?"

She rolls her eyes before looking at Emmie. "Can you believe this one? She's the weirdo that keeps stumbling upon bodies and *I'm* the one with the human head in a bag?" she balks as she pulls the bag onto her lap. "It's just a few clothes I threw together for Juniper Moonbeam. My best fuchsia kaftan for the big V-Day dance coming up at the community center and a pair of your father's favorite sweatpants." She tips her head my way. "And believe you me, kid. It wasn't easy getting them off him. By the way, I need to see Jasper about filing assault charges."

"Against my father?"

"Against that broad he's engaged to," she says the word *engaged* in air quotes. "She swatted me out of her room with her broom."

Emmie chuckles. "So Nathan was in Gwyneth's room when you pantsed him?"

Georgie nods. "I was just moving up their plans for the evening. How was I supposed to know the man likes to go commando?"

"*Ugh.*" I slap my hands over my ears and do my best to stave off any visual from popping into my brain. Note to self: Disinfect room twenty-three asap.

"Anyway"—Georgie fiddles with the straps on her tote bag—"Juni requested Nathan's sweats. She said they were her favorite PJ's."

Emmie coos, "That's so sweet. I sure wish I had a boyfriend so I could steal his clothes."

Georgie gives Emmie's own clothes a onceover. "You wish you had a boyfriend so you could *pants* him."

A laugh belts from me. "She's got you there, Em."

"Ha ha." Emmie does a double take at something near the door. "Excuse me. I think I'm going to head to the restroom."

She takes off and Georgie looks into her tote bag and screams before shutting it tight.

"What?" I squawk, nearly falling off my chair. "Geez, Georgie, you gave me a heart attack. What did you see in that bag of yours? And it had better not have a story about my naked father attached to it."

Her eyes grow wide. "I saw a head!"

"A what?" I pull the bag forward and peer inside and a tiny yelp comes from me. "Georgie!" I hiss as I pull the tote bag onto my lap. "You have Cinnamon in there." I pull the tote bag open just a notch for her to see me, and *breathe.* "What are you doing here, you little cutie pie?"

I curled up in a comfy pair of sweats while I was at Georgie's and I must have fallen asleep.

The next thing I knew that wild woman was screaming at me.

A moan comes from me. "Georgie, it sounds like you must have scooped her up when you picked up the sweats."

She makes a face. "I thought they seemed extra sweaty."

The bartender comes by and we each put in an order for a drink. Georgie opts for a shot of whiskey, and I opt for something fruity and virgin, picking up a fruity virgin delight for Emmie as well.

"Don't worry, Cinnamon," I say to the adorable pup curled up in my lap—albeit in the warmth and safety of that tote bag. "We shouldn't be that long. I'll have you back in my cottage in no time. I bet Sherlock and Fish really miss you."

"Pish posh." Georgie pulls a wad of meat from her pocket and lands it in the tote. "That little redhead is my new best friend." Her phone pings. "Speaking of new best friends"—she glances to the screen—"Juniper Moonbeam is about to make a landing. She's less than a mile away!"

"I'm really happy for you, Georgie." I give a quick glance around and a breath gets caught in my throat. "That's him!" I hiss. "The dark-haired man in a suit with the pointed chin and gold cufflinks. He's near the doorway." Colt stands holding an amber-colored drink as he talks to one of the waitresses. "Save my seat, Georgie. I'll be right back."

Reflexively, I pull the tote bag over my shoulder and head his way with Cinnamon in tow.

It's probably for the better. There's no telling what hysterics will break out once Juniper Moonbeam hits ground zero. For as long as Georgie has lived with me at the Country Cottage Inn—and it's been over four years—that little Moonbeam of hers hasn't paid her a single visit. In all fairness, Georgie and I have never discussed what her relationship was like with her daughter, but I'm guessing it wasn't a good one.

The waitress takes off and I step it up, landing before him as if I were the defense trying to keep the ball from running down the field.

"You look familiar!" I'm really going to have to add a little variety to my interrogation game. "Didn't we meet that night at the Country Cottage Inn?" I grimace to emphasize the nature of the night at hand.

Colt leans back, examining me from head to foot. He's a handsome man by anyone's standards, but there's something hard in his eyes that lets you know there are dirty dealings going on in that head of his.

Speaking of which, I do my best to focus in on his thoughts.

Pretty lady. I wouldn't kick her out of bed for eating crackers.

I all but roll my eyes. This is exactly why I don't make it a habit to pry into anyone's mind. Typically, when someone is having thoughts of the lusty variety, their mind goes straight to white noise. And the fact his hasn't probably signifies his thoughts aren't all that bad.

And just like that, it's snowing behind those glazed-over eyes of his.

Perfect.

I've got a pervert on my hands and I'm his mental victim.

"That's right. We did meet...the night of the murder." I get right to it as Cinnamon begins to squirm before poking her head out the top of the tote.

"Geez." He jolts as if I had garnered the power to electrocute him with my words.

Hey! I know him! Cinnamon gives an odd little moan.

"Yes." I turn my body, hoping he won't see that I'm toting Lad Warner's dog around with me. "That night was pretty horrible."

Bizzy, he tried to help Lad. In fact, he was always helping Lad.

I bet he was. With *bad* loans.

Colt squeezes his eyes shut tight and the white noise dissipates as if on demand.

"I still can't believe he's gone," he says. "Lad was family. I guess you never know how long someone's got. Appreciate the people in your life." He leans in. "What was your name again?" He's scrutinizing me with his eyes. *I don't trust anyone. And I don't think I'm getting a good feeling about her.*

A breath hitches in my throat. "I'm here with my friends." I'm quick to point over to Georgie. "That's one of them. Her daughter just got out of prison and she wanted to meet up with us here." That's right. I'll throw the whole Conner clan under the bus if I have to. "This must be quite a place." If I've learned anything, I've learned that I'm much better at telling the truth than I am at telling a lie. People can sense something is off even with the tiniest deviation from gospel.

His entire body relaxes. "This is quite a place." A smidge of pride takes over his face. "I should know. I'm a half owner." *All right. She's a good egg. I need to chill. Not everyone is working to take me down.* "So any word on who killed Lad?"

I shake my head. "In fact, when I realized who you were, I thought you might have those answers. You mentioned you were family."

"By marriage. But the family doesn't understand it either. It's a real head scratcher."

A tiny bark comes from my bag. *Ask him about the ways he used to help Lad. Sure, they argued some, but then, Lad argued with just about everyone. Except for me. He was kind and gentle, even when I had what he called accidents all over the house.*

Colt cocks his head, his eyes flashing from side to side. "Did you hear that? It sounded like a bark."

"It's just the music," I say. "I think it's some new record spinning technique. Very annoying. I keep thinking I hear a dog barking, too."

He squints over at me. "Maybe. I don't listen to that junk. I'm a smooth jazz man myself. But my cousin, Marty, likes the atmosphere to be popping, so I let him pick the music."

"Did Marty know Lad?"

"Everyone knew Lad."

"Oh right. That explains all the people stopping by the inn to leave flowers by the fountain."

"Really?" he looks stunned by this floral revelation. "That's nice."

"Yes, it is." It's also not true—with the exception of one person, but it does help segue into my next line of thought. "Natalie came by." I let it sink in a moment. He wasn't her biggest fan the night of the murder. "And some man who said he was his bookie." The lie came out just as easy as the truth.

"James?" He leans back in disbelief. "The guy's in Vegas."

Shoot.

I offer up a casual shrug. "Come to think of it, he might have said these are from his bookie."

"That's more like it. And Nat, huh?" He shakes his head at the thought. "That was his ex. They were together a long time. I thought they were lifers. But they weren't the best for one another."

That night at the inn I distinctly remember Colt thinking that Natalie was a bag of trouble. That she and Lad were good for one another. That Colt, himself, still wished they were together. And not only that, but that he still wished he and Natalie were still together, too. It sounds like Natalie Weiland really gets around.

"Did they argue a lot?" I do my best to prod while Cinnamon begins to wiggle like mad.

He winces. "No, it wasn't that. Natalie didn't like how he was handling his finances. She was the more levelheaded between the two. But she was insecure—always thinking she was about to be replaced. It's what made Lad walk away. A guy can only take so many accusations." *It's what made me walk away, too. But, in my case, the accusations were true. I never said I was an innocent man. I'm pretty sure if this little hottie knew what I was capable of, she wouldn't be batting those baby blues my way. Little does she know, she could ask for the numbers on my credit card and I would give them to her. I couldn't deny this little cupcake a single thing.*

Good to know, Colt. I bat my lashes up at him. *Because I'm about to ask for the holy grail.*

"Natalie mentioned something about you loaning Lad money. That was very nice of you." I bite down on my lower lip flirtatiously. "It's a rare man who has spare change to lend out to those in need."

His chest expands with pride. "Lad didn't need it. Not in the way he thought. But we're family. I would have given him more money if he thought it could help." *At thirty percent interest, how could I not?* "But Natalie?" he glowers at the exit a moment. "He was better off without her. Emily—that was his new fiancée." His eyes enlarge for a moment. "I'm sorry. I still don't understand what was happening there. She was a nice lady. Her daughter was a pistol. But that whole relationship sort of came out of left field."

I nod as if I felt the same way. "Natalie said he was in it for the money." Here's hoping the shark and the bookworm don't exchange notes. "From what I understand, he had a pretty bad gambling problem. Money leaking from his bank account like a sieve. And if Emily has anything, it's money."

"You're not wrong there." He sighs. "Lad had a good heart and a brain full of mush. Actually, I take that back. He was a smart man—too smart for his own good. That's what a gambling addiction does to you. It convinces you that the next win will be all you need. And that it will be your last bet. But it never works out that way. Humans are a greedy bunch."

Cinnamon lets out a riotous bark, and this time Colt all but spins me around.

"Whoa, you got a dog in there?"

"I'm sorry. I didn't even realize he was with me until it was too late."

Holy heck. He squints over at Cinnamon and reaches out to pet him.

His eyes flash my way. "This is Lad's dog, isn't it?"

"What?" My heart jackknifes. He's going to think I'm some sort of freak, stalking Lad from the grave. A morbid groupie obsessed with a corpse. "No. Actually, it's from the same litter. A friend of mine had them and Lad took the runt. This is Rusty. I got the pick of the litter. But in truth, they were all so adorable I had a hard time deciding which."

Nice save, Bizzy. Just for the record, I'm a rather proud runt.

I crimp a smile her way. She should be proud. In my eyes, she *is* the pick of the litter.

"That makes sense." He gives Cinnamon a scratch on the head. "You're a sweetheart. Typically, it's a no pets allowed policy, but I'll let you slide anytime."

"Thank you. There's a Valentine's Day dance out in Cider Cove on the fourteenth. If you're in the area, you should stop by. There will be more than enough single ladies to go around. A handsome guy like you shouldn't spend Valentine's Day alone." And that way if I need to question him again, we'll come by it much more naturally.

"Maybe I will." His cheek flinches. "It wouldn't hurt to meet a decent girl for a change." ***And scoring with one on Valentine's Day would be a nice touch.***

"Nice touch?" I balk.

He inches back. "Excuse me?"

Someone calls his name from behind and he turns to leave.

"Wait, Colt? Who do you think did this to Lad?"

"I don't know. But I can tell you right now. I wish he was alive because he owed me a hell of a lot of money." ***And once he paid me back, I'd kill him as a favor to him. The guy didn't know when to quit. He was either destined for prison or the grave. Score one for the Grim Reaper.*** "You know, I'd look into the daughter of his fiancée if I were the homicide detective. She hated the guy. I mean, she's an obvious suspect." *Then there's Madeline. His hot side piece. She was quirky but didn't strike me as trigger-happy. And Emily. Smart lady. She was bound to find out Lad and Nat were back on. Now that would make her trigger happy.* "I'll catch you later. Nice seeing you."

I suck in a quick breath.

Could Emily have found out that Nat and Lad were back on? Nat didn't seem to think they were back on, but she did mention they were seeing one another toward the end. That sounds like back on enough for me—and maybe Emily, too.

He takes off toward the foyer.

"Don't forget about the dance!" I shout after him, but I'm drowned out by the music.

So Natalie and Lad were back on. I wonder how "on" they were? And I wonder if that's what Emily discovered right before Lad was killed? That would have sent any fiancée through the roof. But the gun—I mean, I guess it could have been hers. Nobody is out of the running just yet.

I'm about to head back to Georgie when I spot a woman from behind who looks all too much like my not-so-levelheaded bestie. She's got her arms wrapped around some random man, stuffed in a flannel shirt, and she's kissing him as if he were leaving on the mission to colonize Mars.

"Oh my God." I stalk over and pluck her loose. "Emmie, have you lost your mi—"

And just like that, I lose my own mind.

"*No!*" I shout so loud, I'd swear the walls just rattled—heck, Mars just rattled.

Not only was Emmie making out like there was no tomorrow, but the recipient of that otherworldly kiss was none other than Deputy Leo Granger.

An incredulous growl rips from me. "I do not know who to swat first," the words hiss from me. "What are you doing!" I pull Emmie toward me so I can both protect her and slap her silly. She'll thank me for *both* come morning. "Are you crazy? You're going to get us killed! Mackenzie is going to lose her mind when she finds out you've swiped her boyfriend from under her."

Emmie shakes her head frenetically. "Leo says they're not serious."

"I don't care what Leo says. I can guarantee you, Leo is not in charge of that relationship. Mackenzie is going to scalp us in the night. Or worse, she's going to find a much more creative way to make us suffer. And make no mistake about it. She'll include me in on the fun." I turn to Leo and glower. "This is all your fault. I saw how you were looking at my bestie back at the café. I should have squashed this like a bad love bug while I had the chance."

Leo opens his mouth to say something when a blonde woman with long scraggly hair, a bright blue kaftan, and flip-flops bounds in with her hands waving over her head as she screams with delight all the way over to Georgie.

"I think we've just had a moon landing," I say to no one in particular before looking back to Emmie and Leo. "How about we chalk this whole night off to one big galactic hallucination? Got that, Leo? That kiss never happened. As you were with Mayor Woods. God knows if she gets wind of this, your bits and pieces are on the chopping block."

He cinches his legs a notch—as he should.

I pull Emmie over with me as we head back to the bar, and Cinnamon hikes up on her hind legs to get a better look at the world around her.

Is that Georgie's puppy?

"That would be her," I say, only vaguely recalling the woman from that all too brief matrimonial encounter she had with my father. She looks younger, if that were at all possible. Her face is round and wrinkle free, her bright blue eyes have that same touch of mischief as Georgie's carry, and her accouterments—it's safe to say the kaftan fruit didn't roll far from the hippy tree.

Georgie and Juni eventually slow their show-stopping squeals and rather aggressive embraces—although, if I just got out of prison, I would have held onto my mother in the exact same way.

"Bizzy!" Georgie pulls me in. "You remember Juniper Moonbeam. Juni, can you believe our little Bizzy Baker is all grown up? And this is her best friend, Emmie." She pulls Emmie in close.

Juni squints over at me as if she were having a hard time placing me, and I don't blame her. It feels as if it's been a decade if it hasn't been two.

"Hello, girls!" She laughs as she pulls Emmie and me into a strangulating embrace. "To the four musketeers! Now who's buying? It's not every day you get released from prison, you know. I say we move right past the whiskey and head straight for the champs. None of that carbonated vinegar they sell you for ten bucks a bottle, either. I prefer me some Dom."

Georgie whoops and hollers, and soon the bartender is sending a steady stream of 100 proof poison our way. Georgie and Juni get schnockered while I hold Cinnamon at a safe distance. And all the while, Emmie is having unholy thoughts about Leo Granger that I would give anything not to pry into.

Cinnamon reaches up and licks my cheek. *Take me home, Bizzy. This place is for the birds—loud, angry birds.*

Much to her delight, Emmie and I collect a couple of happy drunk birds called Georgie and Juni and hightail it all the way back to Cider Cove.

It's time to catch a killer.

And I think Emily Carter has some explaining to do.

13

True to his word, Jasper stopped by last night for dessert. Lucky for me, I was fresh out of those raspberry bite-sized cheesecakes and we had to get creative. Suffice it to say, the furry folks among us ran for cover once they saw just how creative Jasper and I could be.

I couldn't help it, though. Jasper is a man's man. A man among men. A deity in the flesh. And who am I to turn down those kissable lips? Those strong arms? That sexy maneuver where he—

"*Bizzy*?" a female voice shrills from behind just as I'm about to hop into my car, and I turn to find my worst nightmare barreling in this direction.

"Mayor Woods." I straighten. It's about two in the afternoon and I left Nessa and Grady in charge of the inn. Georgie and Juni were more than glad to take charge over

Fish and Cinnamon, while Jasper took Sherlock to work again. And according to his thoughts, it has more to do with warding Camila off than it does his desire to sneak Sherlock a steady stream of donuts throughout the day.

Mackenzie's eyes glow like fire as she strides on over as if she were about to walk right through my car.

"What's going on with Leo?" she growls out the words.

"Excuse me?" I do my best to blink back surprise. But it's no use. As much as I can read minds, Mack here can read body language. In fact, she might be better with her gift than I am with mine.

She cinches her glossy lips. Her arms fold across her chest, pulling at that siren red power suit she's donned. It must be miserable dressing up for corporate America every single day, only to roam the mean streets of Cider Cove. It wouldn't hurt her to throw a sweater into the mix once in a while. But, for some reason, Mackenzie has always tied together fashion and power. She's not necessarily wrong in doing so. I'm just glad I have a job where a sweater and my favorite fuzzy boots are perfectly acceptable attire.

"Something is up." She glares at the inn as if it were to blame. That is, unless she can sense Emmie's presence. Dear God, I had better warn my bestie that Mack is on the prowl, and she's baring her fangs—a surefire sign that she means business. "I think it's Camila. She's up to her old wicked reindeer games again. So I did the only thing I could think to do."

"You slaughtered them both in their sleep?" Cider Cove has been a bit homicide happy in the last few months. I'm not entirely sure I could blame her.

"I dumped him."

"You dumped Leo?" I inch back to get a better look at this once-upon-a-best-friend of mine. "Like this morning?" Inquiring minds want to know. If that's the case, Mack is far more intuitive than I give her credit for.

"Like yesterday." She sags as her expression goes from rage to self-pity, a psychological pit stop Mackenzie Woods isn't all that familiar with. And my guess is, she doesn't much care for it.

"Yesterday?" I balk as I do the make-out math. "Like, say, before five in the afternoon?"

She gives a quick nod. "Yesterday morning to be exact. I brought him breakfast down at the station and found Camila sitting on his desk like some 1950s pinup girl. It made me sick, so I gave him the boot."

"What?" I balk at the thought of Mackenzie Man Eater Woods reacting in such a knee-jerk manner. "Mack, you and I both know Camila has an unnatural attraction to office furniture. It's exactly why she lost her last job." It's true. Camila worked for the school district out in Sheffield right before they found out she took a bunch of naughty photos while posing with innocent slabs of mahogany. "I can't believe you fell for that."

She flinches as if I struck her. "You're right. I should probably talk to Leo. It's not too late. I mean, it's not like he went out last night and made out with some tramp in a dive bar."

She had the dive bar part right.

But Emmie is no tramp.

"Thank you, Bizzy." She gives her rosy lapels a quick tug. *I miss this. I miss her.* She sighs. *And for some reason, I knew she could make things better.* "I'll see you at the Valentine's Day event next week." She stalks off to wherever she parked her broom. "Double the order for the cheesecake bites! It's on the city's tab."

I climb into my car and pause for a moment to catch my breath.

I don't think I made things better. If anything, I've made things worse.

I'll have to talk to Emmie once I get back.

But first, I'm picking up my sassy sister and we're headed to Carter Art Corporation headquarters to look at those dicey paintings I've heard so much about.

"Why am I here again?" Macy applies another swipe of hot pink lipstick solely using the reflection on her phone.

"Because Georgie's puppy came home to roost," I say. "Juniper Moonbeam has planted herself at the inn. Do you remember her?" I ask as I look over at the Carter Art Centers' corporate offices in the distance, a pale blue building with giant canvases covered in pink and purple hearts decorating the expansive windows.

"Looney Juni?" Macy teases. "How can I forget? I was the flower girl at the marital fiasco. You passed out on the lawn after eating too much of their cotton candy wedding cake and Mom threatened to sue the new Mrs. Baker for child endangerment. She said your adult teeth were destined to turn to chalk."

"That explains a myriad of things," I say, ironing out the front of her lavender blazer with my hands. "Exactly how many power suits do you have, and since when did Mackenzie Woods become your fashion guru?"

She makes a face and flicks my hands away. "For your information, Mom is my fashion guru. When she quit the glitz and glamour of small-town real estate, she bequeathed her power suit collection to me and I gladly accepted. And by the way, Mayor Woods took a page out of Mom's look book." She says *Mayor Woods* in air quotes.

"What makes you think that?"

"She told me. She said she's always admired what a strong woman our mother was. And when she was running for mayor, she adopted her sense of style and her hardnosed public relations persona."

I pause for a moment as I let this sink in.

"You mean, Mack has been running around all this time doing a terrible impression of our mother?"

Macy shrugs. "Can you blame her? Mom has always been our fearless leader."

"I guess I can't blame her." I try my best to shake all of that weirdness out of my head. For so long Mackenzie has treated me as if I *killed* her mother, and here she's been worshiping at the altar of mine. "Let's get in there. I'm ready to do this thing. Try not to break anything, would you?"

"The only thing I'm looking to break is my record."

A dull moan expels from me. "Do I want to know?"

She makes a face my way. "My record for how many numbers I can collect. Everyone knows there's nothing hotter than a mysterious artist who's looking for his muse."

I make a face right back at her.

"What?" She laughs. "I happen to look good in the nude."

"I've heard enough." I link my arm through hers as we head on in. "Remember, big sisters are better seen and not heard. Work actively not to get us kicked out on our ears, would you?"

"Will do. Just remember, you invited me to this party."

Inside, the building has an airy appeal with cavernous ceilings and a modern staircase that looks to be pieced together with acrylic and string that leads up to a second level. The secretary out front quickly points us in that direction once I tell her I was invited to ogle the artwork in the boardroom, and Macy squeezes the life out of my arm all the way up.

"I did not sign up for some hippy skywalk experience," she whimpers as she closes her eyes. "My God, they should have had us sign a waiver. Bizzy, if I fall to my death, I want you to sue their pants off."

"I'm not suing their pants off—because you're not falling to your death. You can open your eyes now. We've arrived at our destination," I say in the same monotone style as the navigation device in my car.

The second level holds more of a corporate appeal with its isolated cubicles and rows of walled off offices.

Just as I'm about to ask someone for assistance, a small crowd emerges from a set of double doors to our left.

An entire mob of well-dressed men and women stalk out with long faces as they whisper amongst themselves, and I can hear a few errant thoughts.

Emily Carter is a wicked witch if ever there was one.

And to think Paige promised us change if she ever succeeded in giving Lad the boot. And here he's dead and nothing has changed.

I need to get some chowder in me, start a fire, and contemplate the sad state of my life. Maybe it's not too late for a career change? I hear political PR has its charms. It couldn't be worse than this.

I pull Macy in. "It looks as if their corporate meeting just got out."

Macy nods. "And by the looks of things, it didn't go well." She gasps as she glances to our left. "A bunch of them are heading off to that room down there. I can see coffee, cookies, and hot men. It's a trifecta of perfection. I'll see you later, Bizzy. Good luck catching your killer." She stalks off and I'm about to protest when Paige steps out of the boardroom and lands her gaze right on me.

"Bizzy?" A genuine smile comes to her lips. "I'm so glad you could make it." Her entire face opens up with surprise.

"Thank you," I say as I make my way over to her. Her pale blonde hair is pulled back into a low bun and she's wearing a tweed power suit, a trend I seem to be missing out on. "I was just in the area and my curiosity got the better of me."

"Your timing is perfect. My mother is here. You remember her from that night, don't you?"

"Oh, that's right. I do," I say as my heart thumps wildly. Emily Carter just so happens to be the exact woman I want to talk to and it looks as if it's my lucky day.

"In fact, she's right inside talking to someone who's working on the case."

"Case?" I ask just as I step into the spacious boardroom, only to freeze solid once I spot a rather brawny looking homicide detective and his very pregnant sister— who happens to be a curator of fine art, standing right beside them. "Oh no," I whimper as I do my best to shrink out of existence.

Ella spots me first. She's so adorable with her standard Wilder issued face. No kidding, all of the Wilder siblings are basically knockoffs of one another, same dark hair, same pale gray eyes. Ella is a stunner, and her pooched belly is adorable as can be. I happen to know she's due at the end of next month.

Her eyes grow wide.

"Bizzy?" Her mouth rounds out a laugh, interrupting the conversation Jasper was knee-deep in with Emily Carter.

The three of them look my way and Jasper's eyes grow in size, matching his sister's.

"Bizzy." He says my name as if it was a fact he was resigned to, and his lids hood a notch. *How did I not see this coming? But, then again, one of the things I like best about her is her ability to surprise me. Although, this shouldn't have surprised me. I should have preempted this. In the future, I'll do just that. Bizzy Baker doesn't realize it yet, but I'm about to handcuff her from endangering herself in any more investigations.*

I scoff over at him without meaning to. Okay, fine. I so meant to.

"Hello," I force the word out brightly. "Paige had invited me to come out and see the artwork. Georgie, too, actually, but her daughter is in town and she couldn't make it. She asked if I'd take pictures."

Someone calls for Paige from behind and she groans.

"Excuse me, Bizzy. I'll be right back, but I'm sure my mother will be glad to show you the display." *I hope the three of them laugh in her face. A quarter of a million dollars could have bought something real, not some worthless pieces of art.*

She takes off and I gasp at the revelation.

A quarter of a million dollars?

Emily must have been out of her mind to shell out that kind of cash.

"Hi, Emily," I say warmly as I stride their way. "We met at the inn that night. I'm sorry for your loss."

The older blonde gives a mournful nod. "It's been an adjustment." *One I can live with.*

Ella pulls me into a warm embrace. "It's so nice to see you, Bizzy."

"And you look great." I glance down at that basketball she has tucked under her shirt. "I bet you can't wait to hold your little one soon."

She lands her hand on her belly and groans, "It won't be soon enough."

Emily gives a warm laugh. "I remember that feeling. There are some moments in life that just can't seem to get here fast enough. Like the birth of a baby, or a wedding."

Or a death, but that came surprisingly on time.

I clear my throat. "That must be especially hard for you," I tell her. "I mean, you were about to get married yourself."

She takes a quick breath. "I've spent all week canceling venues now that he's gone." *Of course, after what I heard, I would have canceled them regardless.*

Knew it. She did hear something that night, and that's what sponsored the argument and perhaps the fatal gunshot.

Jasper tips his head thoughtfully. "I'm sure that couldn't have been easy. When was the wedding due to happen?"

"Spring—first week of May to be exact." Emily sags with the thought. "But now I'll spend spring alone." *As I should have all along. And so will he, just the way he deserves to.* "Lad was a good man. It's too bad his life was cut short. In those few months I knew him, he made me feel like the queen of the world. I would have given him anything and often did." She raises a hand to the row of acrylic and oil paintings behind her, all on a uniform canvas about four by six feet. They run a rainbow of colors, each one washed in one basic hue with paint running down the front along with a few splatters ala Jackson Pollack. I can see why Paige wasn't that impressed with them, especially if they're from a virtually unknown artist.

Ella shakes her head. "Emily? Tell us what you know about the artist." *I won't have the heart to tell her my true thoughts on these disaster pieces.*

Emily laughs. "Detective Wilder says you're the professional. All I know is that they're from someone named Land Wei. It sounded exotic enough. He's got a gorgeous website, stunning reviews, but I've never heard of him."

"That's strange," I say. "I mean, you're in the art world. I would think you would have heard of just about everyone."

She twitches her lips. "Not true. I specialize in turning a profit out of art classes. I'm far from a connoisseur. But Lad loved them. That's what drew me to him initially— his love for the creative side of life." *He was creative himself come to find out. That little tart of his thought she would wait in the wings until they sucked me dry. I couldn't be more thankful that she showed up that night—that my courage showed up that night.* "But now that he's gone, I'm going to replace these with something more my style."

She's thankful that her courage showed up that night? As in showed up to kill Lad?

My eyes lock over Jasper's with concern.

Bizzy Baker. He sighs as a soft smile plays on his lips. *How I can't wait to get her alone. How I can't wait to show her the surprise I have for her. I hope she likes it. Heck, I hope she loves it.*

My cheeks heat.

Whatever it is he's hoping to surprise me with, I already love it.

Emily takes us from one strange spectacle to the next as Ella gets up close and personal with each one. Her thoughts confirm to me what I already believed to be true. These are nothing more than a farce designed to bilk money from this poor woman.

Hey? I wonder if she knew about Lad's gambling addiction?

"Emily"—I whisper as we step off to the side while Jasper and Ella inspect the final green and blue blotched mess a few feet away—"did Lad have any hobbies other than art?"

She blinks back as if my question caught her off guard.

I give a quick shrug. "I was just thinking maybe someone in the art world, or perhaps someone involved with another one of his hobbies, held a grudge against him and that's who he met up with in front of the inn that night."

"Oh, I don't think so." She's quick to dismiss it. *On second thought, I'd better go with it.* "But you could be right. Lad had two more paintings commissioned and we missed the down payment on both. Apparently, the artist was very angry." She nods to the wall of horrors. "But that was my fault. I was in the middle of inventorying my assets, both liquid and non-liquid. It was a part of analyzing my estate. I was in the throes of rewriting my will, reorganizing who would get what, should I pass one day. Lad did mention the artist had threatened him. Lad tried very hard to get the rest of the money from me, but I stood my ground. I needed time. And am I ever glad I did so." She glances over her shoulder to affirm the fact Jasper and Ella are steeped in conversation. "It turns out, you can't always trust the men in your life. I'm afraid my life has become a cautionary tale."

"What do you mean?"

"My daughter unearthed some disturbing information just a few days ago. There were other women still very much interested in Lad even though we were engaged. I think one of them might have been angry enough to kill."

My lips part as I examine her. "Did you tell the detective?"

She shakes her head. "I'm not ready to face the public with this. It's too humiliating."

"You should. It can be anonymous."

Jasper steps over, his brows hanging crooked over his eyes.

"Ladies." His expression is stone cold. "Everything all right?"

Emily swallows hard, and I nod over at her.

"It's okay," I say. "It's the right thing to do."

"Oh, all right." She shudders. "Detective, after Lad died, I found out through my daughter that he might have been having multiple affairs. I'm afraid one of those relationships may have resulted in his death."

I grill her twice and nothing. And yet I leave her alone with Bizzy for five minutes and she's handing me the keys to the kingdom. I guess I have to give credit where credit is due. Bizzy really is that good.

Jasper leans her way. "Do you know who they could be?"

Emily pulls her shoulders back, her lips pulling in a tight line. "An old friend of his, Natalie Pyle, and possibly one of my employees, Madeline Harper."

Natalie *Pyle*?

Jasper jots it down in this phone. "I'll look into both of those women. Thank you for letting me know your suspicions."

"Oh, they're not suspicions." Emily growls out an incredulous laugh. "I found evidence at my home. That's where Lad had been staying on and off. I found an earring that didn't belong to me in my guest room—the bed looked poorly made. But Lad said the housekeeper must have taken a nap. I knew she didn't, but I played along. Anyway, my daughter said she had it on good authority that those women were very much seeing my fiancé." She glowers at the wall behind me. "And now he's dead." *And I don't feel sorry for him in the least.* "Excuse me." She touches her hand to her chest. "I need to go collect myself." She stalks off and a stunned silence crops up in her wake.

Jasper leans in, bearing those icy eyes into mine.

"Bizzy Baker, I thought we had an understanding?"

"What was that, Detective?"

His features soften. "That I escort you to speak with a suspect."

"And as fate would have it, you are."

He closes his eyes, and I swear on all that is holy, the lights in the room just dimmed.

"Jasper"—his name expires from my lungs—"I'm sorry I've disappointed you. It's just—I was invited to look at the art, and I was curious."

"You didn't disappoint me." His hand cups my cheek. "You scared the hell out of me. Bizzy, you came alone."

"No, I promise I didn't come alone. Macy's here. She just so happens to be appreciating art of the human variety in the next room." I frown over at him. "And you brought your sister. I don't remember getting an invite."

"Touché." *And if I tell her why I really brought Ella, it would ruin everything.*

I look up at him through a new lens. I get the feeling Ella has something to do with this surprise he's working on.

Ella strides up. "They're trash." She shrugs. "The poor woman was bilked. If the guy was still alive, I'd suggest she have him arrested. I've never seen anything so blatant. I've taken pictures. I'll ask around. But I'd be very curious to know where he got these."

"Thanks, Ella." Jasper gives her a quick pat on the back. "Let's get you home and off your feet."

We leave the room and run into Macy talking to a tall man in a black turtleneck and sandals.

"Macy"—I do my best impression of a ventriloquist as I say her name—"it's time to say goodbye."

She snarls my way a moment. "And this is my sister, Buzzkill, that I was telling you about. It seems I'm needed. You have my number. Don't waste it."

"You're lovely," I say as I help her back down the invisible staircase.

Once we get outside, Jasper gives Ella the keys to his truck and I give Macy the keys to my car so I can have a private moment with Jasper.

"Try not to leave without me," I say as she traipses off into the lot.

Jasper wraps his arms around me, his warm embrace only rivaled by that warm smile rising at the tips of his lips.

"I'm sorry," I whisper.

And he inches back with a look of dismay on his face.

"Don't apologize." He touches his forehead to mine. "My only concern is for your safety. You're everything to me, Bizzy. And above all, I need to know you're safe." He swallows hard. "And my biggest fear is that I can't protect you." ***Especially from herself.***

My mouth opens to say something in rebuttal, but nothing comes out.

And nothing has to because Jasper comes up with a brilliant solution. He lands his lips over mine and we end the conversation in the very best way.

Jasper is right. My thirst for justice usurps his ability to keep me safe.

But this will be the last time.

The very last time.

I'll stop stepping in front of the proverbial train as soon as I track down Lad Warner's killer.

They shot him at the inn.

I picked up the murder weapon and became a suspect myself.

This isn't just another homicide.

This time it's personal.

14

Juniper Moonbeam is a ball of energy that could rival nuclear fission in both its instability and all around destruction.

Juni, Georgie, and I are all huddled around a table in the Country Cottage Café munching on raspberry cheesecake bites like they were about to go out of season. It's a bit unnerving to see this younger version of Georgie with their matching wild hair, albeit blonde to Georgie's gray, same wily eyes, and same Rolodex of exaggerated expressions. I don't remember much from Juni the first time around, but on this go-round it's unmistakable that the fun-loving fruit didn't fall far from the kooky tree.

In the corner of the café, Emmie and Leo Granger have the nerve to whisper amongst themselves. Emmie has even let an errant giggle or two stream from her lips and it's all I can do not to throw a chair in their direction. I've decided the best course of action is to actively ignore them. Hear no evil. Speak no evil. See no evil. And yet whenever I happen to glance that way, Leo doesn't disappear.

I turn my attention back to Juni. "So what exactly were you in prison for again?" I pull Fish onto my lap as we wait for her response together. I seem to vaguely recall Jasper saying something about unpaid parking tickets. Or was it speeding tickets?

She swills the coffee in her hand and it curves over the rim of the mug precariously, splattering onto the floor where Sherlock laps it right up and gags.

Tastes terrible, Bizzy. He growls before doing his best to chase his tail. *I'm sorry they make you drink so much of it.*

"Manslaughter." Juni's blue eyes hang heavy over mine before she bursts out with laughter. "Kidding!"

Georgie fans herself as she sighs with relief and Cinnamon yelps in her lap.

Juni shrugs. "Who the hell knows why they lock pretty girls up in the pokey these days? I'm a divorcee twice over. I haven't had much luck with coloring inside the legal lines. But mmm"—she tugs at her blouse and tests the durability of those buttons as she gazes off to some unknown lusty pasture beyond me—"those prison guards with their sexy muscles, those tight-fitted shirts, those angry, hostile stares. And *ooh* the way they squeezed me tight." She takes a page out of her mother's overheated book and fans herself with her fingers. "I'm about ready for my next trip up the river."

"What?" I squawk, half-afraid she'll empty the registers just to ensure it.

She rolls her eyes. "Please, I'm kidding." That faraway look returns to her eyes. "But what I wouldn't do to get in front of that ornery judge once again. Blue eyes, black hair, and those heavy lids of his as he says *get in my private chambers so I can punish you proper*."

Good heavens. Fish yowls. **Someone toss a glass of water over her. I think she's in heat.**

Cinnamon barks. **Can we have her arrested? I think she agitates Georgie.**

I give a little nod. I think she agitates the free world.

Georgie slams her hand over the table. "Enough of your sparkling love life, Juniper Moonbeam. All that talk of comely prison guards and hot-to-trot judges—it's clear that Bizzy here is getting a wee bit jealous."

Fish chortles and, my goodness, it sounds like a bona fide laugh.

Georgie leans in. "Let's help solve this case so you and Detective Wilder can get a little wild yourselves. What's on the agenda? If anyone here has a criminal mind, it's my Juni."

I won't disagree with her on that.

I proceed to tell them about yesterday's faux pas and how it bristled Jasper's feathers because he's afraid he can't keep me safe.

Juni balks, "If he really wanted to keep you safe, he'd make sure you were packing heat."

"Heat?" I inch back. "As in a weapon?"

Sherlock barks. *I'd talk to Jasper first if I were you. He doesn't even like me touching his no-no.*

In contrast to Sherlock, I'm afraid Jasper will gleefully hand me his no-no. My biggest fear is Jasper being onboard with the idea.

"I don't think I want to buy a gun."

Juni juts her chin out, as if trying to piece together why I would reject such an explosively brilliant idea.

"Why not?" she hoots. "You can pick one up anywhere on the cheap. Like, say, a pawn shop?"

I'm about to shake my head when my mouth falls open.

"Yes," I say. "Like a pawn shop."

Fish meows sweetly. *I wouldn't do it, Bizzy. Cinnamon has been chewing on everything. And no matter how hard I hide my toys, she not only finds them, but she destroys the squeaky. If that gun has a squeaky, it will be toast.*

I have a feeling Cinnamon would be toast if she gnawed on a pistol.

I plant a kiss over the top of Fish's head and set her down next to Sherlock. "I say we pack up these pets and head down to the nearest pawn shop. What do you say, ladies?"

Fish roars. *Count me out, Bizzy. I'll keep the inn safe from predators*. She scampers as fast as she can back toward the reception counter.

Georgie and Juni let out a roar of their own—a roar of approval. The way they're whooping and hollering you'd think we were headed off to have a steamy time with a trio of prison guards.

Georgie stands and links her arm through Juni's.

"Heigh-ho, heigh-ho, to buy a gun we go," Georgie sings while Juni does an odd little constricted hop and skip all the way to the door, a move I'm pretty sure she perfected during her time in shackles.

Cinnamon bops in Georgie's arms while looking back at me. *Hurry, Bizzy! Before they leave without you!*

Sherlock strides by my side as we head their way.

I don't know, Bizzy. I think you should see what Jasper thinks first. I'm not sure if Georgie and Juni are powerful enough to keep you safe.

"Don't worry. I'll make sure Jasper knows all about my little adventure." I'm just not sure if I'll let him in on it before or after it happens.

Besides, I'm not really going to buy a gun.

I'm simply gunning for a killer.

Edison is lovely this time of day. That is, if you're in the mood for a strip club or a dicey weapon that could inflict bodily harm.

The Pawn King is a tiny little nugget nestled between an exotic plants shop and the Liquor Emporium. The sign out front boasts *Pawn with comfort!*

I hold Cinnamon tight as Georgie minds Sherlock on his leash.

Juni takes a look at the sign and lets out a hoot before smacking her mama on the arm.

"Would you look at that?" she honks out the words. "*Comfort.* That means free booze for everyone."

We head on in, and much to my surprise and delight, it's clean and spacious. A large glass counter wraps around the periphery of the shop and there are a few curios that line the middle of the store with odds and ends in them. An armed guard stands at the door with his beefy muscles bulging out of his shirt. And as soon as he spots Juni, his stubbled cheeks hike with a smile as he nods her way.

Georgie groans at the sight of him before smacking her dicey daughter right back.

"Jumpin' Juniper!" Georgie howls. "Would you look at the wall of muscles? Hello"—she staggers forward—"come to Mama."

Juni pulls her back. "Down, girl. I've got dibs on all correctional officers." She wastes no time getting in his face. "If you've got the crime, I can do the time."

Why do I get the feeling that's a line she's used before—*and* it's come to fruition?

"Come on," I say, taking Sherlock's leash from Georgie. "We'll let them duke it out while we solve a crime of our own."

Sherlock moans. *I don't want to get arrested, Bizzy. You don't think Jasper will come here and take us downtown, do you?*

"With my luck? It's hard to say. But don't worry. We should be quick."

Good. Sherlock shudders. *I don't like spending time with that Camila. She sits on Jasper's desk the entire livelong day. And she doesn't have any bacon for me like Georgie, or a kind smile like you do.*

I straighten at the thought of Camila sitting on Jasper's desk all day long like a sexed-up cinder block.

Cinnamon titters. *Oh dear, Bizzy. I can see the jealousy in your eyes. You really do love that man, don't you?*

"I do," I confess. "And I really don't care for Camila. The woman is harder to get rid of than a cockroach."

"Did I hear you say cockroach?" A man behind the counter calls to me with a wave. He's tall and lean, with a long goatee and a friendly looking smile.

I traipse on over with my menagerie.

"Hi, I'm looking for a gun." Words I never thought would come from my mouth.

He squints over at me with a touch of suspicion. "Ever shot one?"

"Nope." I probably should have at least hesitated if I wasn't going to lie.

"Ever held one?" His left brow hikes as if he were amused.

"Nope."

His mouth opens for a moment. "Okay. I'll show you what I got. In fact, I've got a two-for-one special going on right now."

Sherlock vocalizes for a moment. *It sounds like they'd sell one to me if they could.*

Cinnamon chortles. ***They are having a two-for-one special. I can get one, too.***

They've got a point.

The man walks me to the next counter where a plethora of weaponry greets me in the locked glass case beneath the counter.

"I've got Glocks, .38 Specials. You name it. You want something pink and fashionable? I've got that, too. Maybe something short and sassy?"

He points to a tiny gun that looks every bit like a toy my brother once had when we were kids.

Come to think of it, I'm pretty sure they've outlawed those kinds of toys since then, and I can see why.

"You've got quite the selection," I say, looking at them row by row to see if I can find one that looks just like the murder weapon. It might have been dark that night, but when it gleamed in my hand, I memorized it.

"What do you want it for, little lady? You don't look like the type who needs to fire a warning shot or two at a couple of debt collectors. You're too pretty. Too clean." He glances to Cinnamon and Sherlock. "You got well-behaved pets, too. I'm guessing you got an ex after you."

My lips part, but not a sound comes from me. "Something like that," I say. "It's complicated." A thought comes to me. "I work down in Cider Cove. We've been having a rash of homicides." I genuinely shudder. "I just want to keep safe."

"Ooh yeah." His demeanor darkens. "I heard about that. You guys need to hire a SEAL team to keep watch over that sleepy seaside town. I think the crazies are using it as a serial killer training ground."

Both Sherlock and Cinnamon moan.

Good Lord, that fun fact probably has an inkling of truth to it. And then it's as if a heavenly choir bursts out in song.

"This one!" I say, stabbing my finger on the glass over a replica of the exact same gun I held in my hand that night. "Hey?" I pretend to feign surprise. "I think I've seen this gun before. Yes, I have. I saw the sheriff's department handling one just like it the night Lad Warner was killed."

His lids spring wide. "That would be the gun, all right." He gives a wistful shake of the head. "But not this one, of course. The sheriff's department is probably going to let the murder weapon rot in an evidence drawer somewhere. A shame when you think about it. A perfectly good weapon gone to waste."

"Yes, well, it killed a person. It probably deserves to rot," I say it low as if I were whispering to Cinnamon and she gives a soft bark right back.

I couldn't agree more, Bizzy.

My arms tighten around her before I lean in toward my new friend, the pawn king.

"So you know all about the gun?" I ask as I tilt my ear his way. "Who do you think purchased the weapon? I mean, an upright organization such as yourself probably has a record of it, right?"

He bats a hand through the air. "I don't have time for recordkeeping. You buy one of these pretties, I'll promise to zip my lips."

"Great," I mutter. "I mean, *great*." I force a smile. "Who needs records? Someone as handsome and smart as you probably has the ability to practically memorize what you sell and to whom." I let the ego stroke sink in and watch as a wide smile spreads across his face. "Hey, you wouldn't by chance remember who bought that gun, would you? I bet you do," I say. "I bet you recall it with crystal clarity."

"That I do." He doesn't hesitate with the answer. "I can tell ya"—he leans across the counter, his marbled green eyes bearing hard into mine—"but then I'd have to kill ya."

Both Sherlock and Cinnamon break out into a series of semi-aggressive barks.

"Whoa whoa," he bellows it out with laughter. "Call off the cute cavalry. I'm just kidding. I wouldn't hurt your mama for nothin'. Especially after I sell her one of these babies." He points to the glass case. "And as for that other gun, it was the dead man himself who came in and bought it."

"What?" It squeaks out of me with surprise. "It was Lad himself?"

"Yup. And now he's dead as a doornail. I'm telling you, I don't sell toys. You put one of these in the wrong hands and things can go very wrong for *you*."

"Like it did for Lad," I pant, suddenly struggling to catch my breath. "Did he say why he needed the gun?"

His eyes travel toward the ceiling. "He mentioned it was for his friend, an artist. He wanted her to have protection."

"Was he alone when he made the purchase?"

He glances to the ceiling. "Nope. He had a brunette cutie much like yourself with him that day. I've seen her around town a time or two."

Madeline? She has brown hair and blue eyes just like me and happens to work just down the street at the art center. He could have easily seen her around town a time or two.

He shrugs. "I already told the detective that came nosying around here all of that. Still no arrest, though. I guess it wasn't such a big break in the case."

A brief prickling runs through me. "You told the homicide detective in charge?"

"That would be him. Detective Jasper Wilder. Talked to him a few days ago."

I swallow hard.

How do you like that? Jasper's been sitting on a wealth of information and he didn't bother to share. Not that I expect him to.

Sherlock and Cinnamon get antsy, and I thank the man before tearing Georgie and Juni down from Mount Muscles.

"Where to now, Bizzy?" Georgie shouts as we make a break for the car.

"The art center down the street. I'm either going to meet with the killer or she'll lead me right to them."

Either way, Madeline Harper, I'm coming for you.

15

Lucky for me, the Carter Art Center is located just a hop
and a skip away from the Pawn King. And lucky for Georgie
and Juni, this sip and paint has a live model—a man of a
certain age, who is currently deprived of a single stitch of
clothing. He's surrounded by heart-shaped mylar balloons,
a couple of lit candles, and a box of chocolates in one of
those fancy velvet heart-shaped boxes next to him.

"Oh, Juniper Moonbeam!" Georgie cries out as she
strangles Juni's arm. "You've always been my good luck
charm."

The entire class begins to giggle just as Madeline
Harper quickly strides this way.

"Bizzy!" She gives a cheery wave. "Three of you
today?"

"Oh, we haven't paid." I shake my head her way as if declining the offer.

"You can ante up afterwards." She motions for us to follow her. "And the dogs are welcome to stay." She takes Cinnamon from my arms as she seats us in the right-hand corner, a little too close to the fleshy subject matter at hand for my liking, but the rest of my party seems pleased.

Sherlock whimpers as he spins in a circle. *Why isn't that man wearing any clothes, Bizzy?*

Cinnamon whines as well. *Why is he covered with fur? And what a small tail he has—in front, no less.*

Oh good Lord. I turn my head toward Madeline until I'm practically facing the opposite direction of the furry subject at hand.

Georgie and Juni get right to work, sketching, mixing their acrylics, imbibing.

"Sorry about the other night." I wrinkle my nose at the adorable brunette. "My sister has never been able to hold her liquor."

"Don't worry about it. We get a live one at least once a week. She helped us meet our quota." She nuzzles her face into Cinnamon's fur and Cinnamon nuzzles right back.

A warm laugh bounces from me. "I'm glad she could help. And since you've met your quota, I'll make sure these girls behave." I nod to Georgie and Juni, each with a glass of wine in hand.

Who knew this day would devolve into day drinking?

Me, that's who.

And ironically, I'm not having a sip.

Madeline giggles into Cinnamon's neck.

"I'm not worried about it, Bizzy. How's everything at the inn? Getting ready for Valentine's Day?"

"Oh, we're ready. I've got the place decorated in more hearts and Cupid cutouts than should ever be legal. And the Country Cottage Café has an entire Valentine's menu plotted out for the day of. Heart-shaped pancakes for breakfast, spaghetti and heart-shaped meatballs for lunch."

"What about dinner?" She blinks my way and there's an innocence about her. She doesn't exactly scream *killer*, but then, if I've learned anything from my past encounters with homicidal maniacs, you can never be too sure.

"The café will be closed for dinner. In fact, the inn will be running with a skeleton staff. Everyone else will be at the community center for Cider Cove's annual Valentine's Day dance. You should really come. It's not far, and there will be lots of eligible men."

Her eyes trail to the door.

How I miss Lad. Who knew some of the best memories I'd ever have would be attained while playing the part of mistress? Not that he was

married. She sighs. ***But he was taken—by two other people.***

"Maybe I will go." She shrugs. "I mean, I guess you never know what will happen. It couldn't get any worse than that singles mingle, blind date with Cupid catastrophe." Her shoulders rise to her ears. "Did they ever catch the killer?" A tiny smile curls at the tips of her lips as if she were keeping a secret and whatever it is, delighted her.

"Not that I know of." I lift a brow her way. "I heard the detective spoke to the guy at the pawn shop down the street." I nod as if insinuating I have a little secret of my own. "It turns out, Lad bought the murder weapon himself. Can you believe it? He bought the very gun that only a few weeks later would be used against him. I wonder who he could have been buying that gun for? Himself? To give to someone as a gift? And if so, it does beg the question—did whoever he gave it to use it against him?"

She sucks in a quick breath. "That's probably exactly what happened."

Sherlock circles around her. ***Let's arrest her, Bizzy. She's getting agitated. Jasper says that's a clear sign of guilt.***

Madeline takes a breath as she stares off past me. "Bizzy, you're not going to believe this, but I—uh, just so happened to be at the pawn shop that day. And since Lad and I were friends—" *I truly hope she's lousy at reading faces. I'll never win an award for lying*. "Anyway, he said he was buying that gun for the special woman in his life—Emily."

"He said that?"

She gives a quick nod. "Apparently, the gun she did own was a little too big for those evening handbags she likes to tote around on fancy nights—sort of like the night he was killed. And I bet either she or her uptight daughter did the deadly deed."

Cinnamon's left ear rises a notch as she groans, *But why would they do it?*

I lean in. "Why would they want to kill Lad? I know you mentioned Paige didn't care for him, but why?"

Her lips twitch as she looks deep in Cinnamon's eyes. "Okay, fine. I'll tell you, but only because you care enough to take care of this little girl right here." She lands a kiss to Cinnamon's nose. "Lad was having an affair."

I raise my brows.

Is she finally willing to admit the affair?

She nods as if she heard me. "It was with his ex, a woman by the name of Natalie Weiland. They were inseparable before he was with Emily, and *during* his time with Emily, too." *During my time with him as well, but I didn't care. I wasn't in it for some matrimonial prize like Emily or Natalie. I was in it for a good time and nothing more.*

Sherlock lands his paw over my leg. *Didn't Emily hear disturbing news that night?*

My lips part as I nod his way. "You know, Madeline, Emily confessed to me that she heard disturbing news just prior to his death. A witness said they were arguing."

She shrugs. "Doesn't surprise me. Natalie was there that night. I saw her myself. It was odd. I mean, she knew Lad would be there. He was a part owner of the Dependable app. And wherever Lad went, so did Emily. But then, maybe Lad invited her like he invited me."

"Emily said she overheard something that was very upsetting. Do you think she may have overheard Lad and Natalie?"

She gives an aggressive nod before biting down on her lip. "I did, too. It was very bad. It's not a shocker that Emily or Paige lost their minds and hunted Lad down."

"Madeline, what did you hear?"

Cinnamon whimpers as she looks up at her. *I'll beg and whine until she delivers, Bizzy.*

I give a slight nod the tiny pooch's way. Animals are far more brilliant than we give them credit for.

"Aww," Madeline coos down at the sweet girl in her arms. "It's almost as if she wants to know herself." She shrugs my way. "I heard Natalie saying something about their plan—and if it was still a-go. Lad assured her that it would only take a few months for Emily to voluntarily hand over her liquid assets before she had the *accident*."

"The accident?" My entire body erupts in shivers. "They were going to kill her."

She gives a single nod. "And as Emily or Paige saw it, the only option was kill or be killed."

"Emily or Paige." I shake my head as all the pieces come together.

The class breaks out into a collective titter and reflexively I look toward the front, only to find Georgie noshing on chocolates while having a conversation with the furry man with a short tail.

Sherlock's ears lift a notch. ***He's about to attack!***

And just like that, Sherlock springs to action, closing the distance in a few quick sprints.

"No!" Juni screams as she races to the scene, accidentally knocking over the candles and throwing herself on top of the poor man. In a quick burst, the left side of Juni's kaftan goes up in flames, and the entire room breaks out into wild screams.

"Juni!" I howl as I leap over furniture, knocking over tables and spilling good wine on my way to her.

Juni twirls in a circle while Georgie whips off her own kaftan and starts beating her with it. The naked man quickly follows Georgie's lead and strips Juni of what's left of her kaftan and someone rushes over with a bucket of water, effectively dousing out the flames.

Juni quickly pats herself down, and to everyone's relief she's come away without so much as a singed eyebrow.

The class breaks out into cheers while I quickly hustle my human and canine circus out of there.

We head back to Cider Cove no worse for wear and with far more answers than I thought I would glean.

Emily and Paige have just moved back to the top of my suspect list.

I'm just inches from getting to the bottom of this.

Whoever killed Lad Warner should be on alert.

Her days of freedom are numbered.

16

The gazebo arrived!

Jordy let me know as soon as I got back to the inn, and I wasted no time in texting Jasper that our picnic was about to come to fruition.

Jasper, being the wise man that he is, picked up enough takeout to feed the entire inn.

"Thiam for Thai?" I ask with a laugh caught in my throat as the far too comely detective strides this way with a happy-go-lucky adorable mutt by his side.

Sherlock barks and both Fish and Cinnamon hop his way to playfully wrestle with him.

"I thought we'd try something different. Chinese from the Wok n' Roll." He winces.

My mouth falls open. "Are we cheating on the Dragon Express?"

"Did I make the right choice?"

"Are you kidding? I love Chinese," I say as I wrap my arms around him. "Almost as much as I love you." I bear into his silver eyes before pressing a molten kiss over his lips. "Let's do this." I grab the blankets I set out and give Grady a wave as we leave him to man the reception counter.

Outside the inn, an icy wind blows that steals the order from my hair. The sky is purple and pink with scattered dark clouds freckling the surface, and the ocean holds a tangerine patina.

Sherlock, Fish, and Cinnamon run on ahead, rolling in the powder white sand as they playfully tug at one another.

Once we crest the evergreens that line the path to the bluff, we see it.

"Oh wow." It comes out in a breath, and it's all I can manage. "Is it real?" I muse. "It's right out of a fairytale."

The glossy white structure itself is massive, at least twenty feet wide, with roses crafted into its ironwork that weave their way throughout it.

Jasper gives my hand a squeeze before pulling it up to his lips and landing a kiss over the back.

"It's perfect," he whispers. "It practically commands magic to happen here."

No sooner does he say those words than Sherlock, Fish, and Cinnamon tumble into the gazebo like one giant ball of fur.

I quickly lay out the blanket and Jasper and I take a seat and dive right into those Wok n' Roll boxes. It's safe to say we have a new favorite when it comes to Chinese food.

I clear my throat as I look to the heart-stopping detective beside me.

"I have a confession to make," I say, my eyes never leaving his.

His lips curl at the edges. "You have indecent plans for dessert?"

"That would be you, and if you play your cards right, I might go along with them."

"Lay it out. I want to know what I'm up against."

I lift a brow. "You went to the Pawn King and got the lowdown on that gun."

His demeanor shifts on a dime. Jasper is not amused.

"That's an odd confession." He leans back on his hands, his hardened gaze locked to mine. "And I'm assuming you know this because you went there yourself. You don't give up, do you?"

Fish yowls. *Now he's catching on.*

Sherlock barks right at her. *He only has her best interest at heart.*

Cinnamon curls up into a ball next to me. *Bizzy wants to catch the killer. How is this a bad thing?*

"How is this a bad thing?" I echo the pretty pooch's sentiment.

"It's not." Jasper flashes an all too brief smile as he leans forward. "Not until you wind up in the morgue."

"Speaking of the morgue, that circles us back to the topic of Lad Warner." I offer a brief smile of my own. "Madeline Harper was with him that day at the pawn shop."

"I know that," he says. "And I also know that Lad bought the gun himself."

"Did you know it was a gift for Emily?"

He shifts my way. "No." His eyes widen a notch as if his horror was growing by the moment. "You spoke with Madeline, didn't you?"

"Yup. It was the nude review down at the art center. You couldn't keep Georgie or Juni away with a flesh-covered stick."

His eyes close a moment. *Would it be selfish of me to hope it was a woman and not a man the three of them got to ogle?*

He takes a breath. "What did you learn?"

"That kaftans burn at an accelerated rate when compared to your run-of-the-mill T-shirt."

A hard groan comes from him. "Please tell me nobody ended up in the hospital."

"Only the poor model's ego. Let's just say all that jumping and screaming wasn't very flattering for the guy."

A dull chuckle comes from him. "Anything else?"

"Yes. Madeline confirmed what Emily said. It turns out, Lad's fiancée did overhear a very disturbing conversation."

He nods. "Emily wouldn't say what it was."

"But Madeline did. She was there as well."

He dips his chin. "Don't keep me in suspense."

"Emily overheard Lad and Natalie Weiland talking about a plan they had in place to suck all the money out of her bank accounts within the next six months. And then Lad said there would be an accident. Emily's life was in danger. That's enough to boil anyone's blood. Not only that, but she heard it on the same night that Lad gifted her the gun. It's a no-brainer. Emily pulled the trigger."

He tips his head to the side. "Paige said she found her mother shaken. If Emily told Paige what she overheard, it might have pushed Paige over the edge. She could have easily gotten ahold of the gun herself."

That afternoon we spent in the corporate boardroom plays back in my mind and a thought comes to me.

"Oh my God, Jasper. That day we were talking to Emily, she said she was sure Lad was having an affair with both Madeline and a woman by the name of Natalie *Pyle*."

He nods. "I caught that, too. I figure it was a flimsy attempt on Lad's part to cover her identity."

I nod. "But why? Everyone knew Natalie was his ex." An entire litany of thoughts tumbles through my mind at once. Natalie Pyle. Natalie Weiland. *Weiland*. That sounds so familiar. Wei— oh my God. "Those paintings... Jasper, they were signed by an artist who goes by the name Land Wei. No wonder your sister had never heard of them. Land Wei isn't an artist. More like a *con*-artist. I bet you anything Natalie Weiland painted those pictures."

He takes a breath and his chest broadens. "Geez." His head inches back a notch. "Maybe so, but there's no way to prove it."

The Atlantic churns and heaves over itself as fresh sea air baptizes us with its brine.

"I bet there's a way." I shake my head over at him. "If Emily pulled the trigger, I think those paintings could prove that she was practically pushed to do it. They're evidence that Lad and Natalie were fleecing Emily Carter. And Madeline herself heard that they were going to cause an accident to kill the poor woman."

For once, I'm not nearly as interested in nailing the killer as I am seeing overall justice brought to light.

"Bizzy," he whispers my name with heavy concern in his tone. "I've got this handled. Trust me. I've already discovered that the farm Lad's grandfather owned was in the black. He was taking bad loans to fund his gambling problem, not for his grandfather. I can support the argument that Emily was being horribly used and perhaps primed for murder. I've got this, Bizzy. Enjoy the inn. Enjoy the safety that your life affords you. Leave this to me. Please."

My mouth parts to give a rebuttal, but nothing comes out.

Jasper pulls me onto his lap and lands a mind-numbing kiss over my lips.

"Let's change the course of this conversation," he whispers right over my cheek. "I need a break from the case. Let's focus on us. How about that secret you promised to tell me? This looks and feels like a special place for divulging secrets. What do you think?"

Fish lets out a roar as if someone just gave her tail a good tug. *Bizzy! This is serious. Are you really going to do it? There's no going back, Bizzy. No going back.*

Cinnamon tucks her nose into her belly. *I can't watch.*

Sherlock lets out a soft bark. *Jasper will only love you more. Don't be afraid. Tell him, Bizzy. Tell him everything.*

I make a face at the gazebo. "I'd utter it if I wanted to ruin the ambience here for good." My lips knot up as I look up at the handsome man before me. "How about we continue that kiss? I think it's supercharging this place with the love and positivity a place like this deserves."

"Then it's our civic duty to continue."

And we do.

Too bad for me, I haven't shared my big bad secret just yet. I'm not sure how Jasper will feel about the telesensual side of me. I'm not even sure how I feel about it.

And too bad for Jasper, I'll be looking into Natalie Weiland once again.

Correction—too bad for Natalie.

The next afternoon, the Water's Edge Bookshop looks like a pale bone juxtaposed against a blood red sky. I don't hesitate heading on in.

It's warm inside, the sweet woodsy scent of the paperbacks enlivens my senses, and I don't waste any time in marching right up to the counter. There is a nice stream of customers in the shop today. Mothers with toddlers, teenagers walking around in mobs, a handful of elderly people each with their noses tucked in a book. There's a huge sale banner over a table near the back wall and a cluster of bodies centered around it like a hive.

A young man carrying a stack of hardbacks almost passes me by as he pauses to look my way. He wears dark-rimmed glasses and an easy smile. His hair is shorn short and is an unmistakable shade of fire engine red.

"Can I help you?" he asks, nearly toppling his load.

"I was looking for Natalie. She was helping me with a...book selection." I lean in. "And offering some sage advice when it comes to my love life."

"She does that a lot." His expression sours. ***Natalie is the last person who should be giving away advice like that. In the least it should come with a warning. Unless, of course, this poor girl is looking to become a mistress. Then, Nat might just have the perfect thing to say.*** "She was on her way out to lunch. But she might still be in the workroom in the back. Go on and see if you can find her."

"Thank you."

So he knows about Natalie? It sounds as if she's blabbed all of her dark secrets to her coworkers. I'll let Jasper know when it's time for Emily to build her defense. Not that I agree with the fact Emily killed Lad in cold blood. But after hearing the things she was subjected to, what jury could blame her? It's clear she was driven by sheer insanity.

What if Jasper was cheating on me? And with Camila, his smarmy ex of all people? And what if I had stumbled upon a nefarious conversation of theirs in an effort to not only drain my bank account, but to off me in an accidental manner?

I'd lose my mind, and a bullet or two. And how easy it would be to do that if Jasper had just given me a gun? Of course, I'd probably point it at Camila first. Heck, I might have stopped there.

I shake the homicidal thoughts out of my mind as I hit the back of the bookshop where the air is a little cooler and the din of voices slowly reduce to a thick silence. A small sign hanging on the door reads *STAFF ONLY*, and the door itself sits slightly ajar.

I give a little knock. "Hello?" I sing. "Uh, I'm looking for Natalie." I take a step into the spacious dark room that looks more like a warehouse and smells like my father's garage.

Stacks of boxes sit scattered around. A small table and battered refrigerator sit near the wall to my right. And to my left, the room seems to go on and on with enough inventory lying around to fill another bookstore.

My feet meander that way without hesitation, and I spot a desk sitting under a broken window that's been poorly mended with duct tape.

Papers cover the dusty desk, there's an electronic time card machine to the right, and a bloated calendar that lies flat against the desk that looks as if an entire pot of coffee got dumped onto it. I run my finger across it just to affirm that it's no longer wet and inadvertently turn a few pages, landing the book on May. A series of lines run through the first two weeks of the month with the words *Natalie's vacation, T&C* scrawled over them.

May?

That's when Emily said she was due to marry Lad. The beginning of May specifically. Natalie's vacation lines up with that.

Huh. Maybe she didn't want to be around to witness the catastrophe? I can understand that. Who would want to see the love of their life marrying someone else? Even if it was for money. And even if you were planning to kill the bride at a later date. I bet that homicidal honor would have gone to Natalie. I'm sure she would be ready to do it regardless. I've never felt sorrier for a killer before more than I do for poor Emily—or Paige. But somehow the spontaneity of it all tells me it was a little more passionate. I'd bet the entire inn it was Emily herself.

The scamper of what sounds like mice comes from my left, and I gasp before heading that way. A shard of light hits over something all the way in the back, something large and white that looks strangely out of place in this cardboard box world. And then I see it for what it is.

"How do you like that?" I pant as I head over and run my hand over the enormous pristine canvas. Next to it lies an opened tackle box brimming with acrylic paint. My hand reaches for the canvas, and I pull it forward to reveal another one the exact size nestled right behind it. But this one isn't blank. It's painted in blues and greens with paint dripping down the left side of it, identical to those paintings back at Carter Corporate. And scrolled across the bottom is the name Land Wei.

A breath catches in my throat, and I pull out my phone and quickly take as many pictures of the scene that I can.

Knew it.

Caught you red-handed, Natalie.

All the evidence to prosecute her for those fake works of art is right here. And even though it's not a crime to sell art, it will help fill out the pieces and *paint* the right picture for Emily.

The sound of a car pulling into the lot behind the bookstore filters in through the window, and I look out to see Natalie getting out of a sedan.

My feet carry me right out of the staff room and back into the bookstore. I'm no longer moved to have a conversation with her. Not yet, anyway.

I head to the front and bump into the redheaded man who helped me out to begin with.

"Did you find her?" he calls out as he moves to the register to help ease the line snaking around the front.

"No, I didn't. I was hoping to talk about art with her, too. I hear she's pretty good."

"Good is questionable. She uses the back room as a studio now and again. Art is in the eye of the beholder, I presume."

"That it is," I say as I speed back into the icy afternoon and jump into my car.

I watch in my rearview mirror as Natalie heads into the bookstore on my heels.

Lad was a monster for what he was doing and about to do to Emily, but Natalie is a special kind of monster, too.

And when Emily goes down, I'll make sure Natalie goes down with her.

I'll admit, there's a thread of excitement in me all the way to the Seaview Sheriff's Department. I know that Jasper didn't want me mingling with his investigation, but he'll practically thank me for what I'm about to tell him.

I park and stride on in, all the while thinking I should have come with a platter of those magical raspberry cheesecakes bites. They'd throw Jasper straight into a good mood, and I wouldn't need to worry about how I was going to segue into this conversation. But then, I can always resort to bewitching him with my mouth. It's been known to work a time or two.

The steely interior is devoid of any homey effect, but there are a smattering of metallic hearts stuck along the walls and it gives this hardnosed place a festive appeal.

"Bizzy?" a familiar voice calls from my right, and I look to find Leo Granger heading this with a quizzical look on his face. "What brings you in?"

"Why?" I smart. "Afraid I'm here to take that nightstick you wield and smack you over the head with it? I'm tempted, you know."

"Oh, I know. I can practically read your mind." He sheds a devilish grin.

"Not funny. I'm here to see Jasper. Do me a favor and stay away from Emmie. If Mackenzie finds out, she'll burn all of Cider Cove down as a means of revenge."

Leo chuckles as he does his best to follow me all the way to Jasper's office. The door is ajar, and the sound of hostile voices rising has me halting at the foot of it.

"We didn't have secrets," a female voice shouts, and I peer in enough to verify it's Camila.

"You had a secret," Jasper tells her. "And he happened to be my best friend. Look, I'm not going around the block with you. Next time you have department business that you need to bring to my desk, find someone else to do it or I'll have you replaced." *I'd do it if I could.*

I exchange a glance with Leo and he shrugs.

Camila gives an incredulous huff. "You said you were ready to get serious with her."

"And as soon as she opens up to me about whatever it is she wants to tell me, I will. And that's all I'm telling you. I don't owe you a timeline of where my relationship with Bizzy is going or how quickly we'll get there."

"I just want to know how much time I have, Jasper." There's a threat in her voice. "You and I belong together. If Dizzy Bizzy can't be an open book to you, then do you really want this woman in your life? Think about it, Jasper. If she really loved you, there wouldn't be any big secret after all these months. She'll never tell you. She will never be honest with you. But with a little counseling, we could go back to the point in our relationship that was bliss."

I don't hesitate stepping into the room. "Was that before or after you slept with Leo?"

Camila looks stunning with her hair swept up and her eyes glowing like coals. I'm sure Camila goes all out while getting ready for work in the morning. Every day is prom for her. And she goes out of her way to look her best in an effort to trap her ex.

Her chest thumps with a laugh. "Good luck, Bizzy." *You'll need it. We just had a very special lunch together.*

My mouth falls open as Leo shuts the door behind her and it's just Jasper and me inside his office.

"Did you have lunch with her—again?" It comes out like a threat, and to be honest, I never meant to say it out loud.

221

Jasper has me wrapped in his arms before I can process it.

He furrows his brows a moment. ***Now, how did she figure that out?*** "Does it count if I'm in the sandwich shop next door enjoying my BLT when she plops in the seat across from me and refuses to leave? In my defense, it took me thirty seconds to do just that."

A dull laugh rattles through me. "She's absolutely insane. How will we ever survive her?"

Jasper shakes his head. "We've already survived her. She just hasn't gotten the memo." His lids hood dangerously low. "Your cheeks are rosy. Your eyes shine like pale blue diamonds. You're downright gorgeous, Bizzy Baker." ***I say secret be damned. I'm ready to share my surprise with this beautiful woman. The sooner, the better.***

I clear my throat and press my hands to his chest as if I were about to push him away.

"I'm ready, Jasper. I'm ready to tell you my secret."

"Here?" He gives a quick glance around as if he knows on some intrinsic level this isn't the ideal spot.

I give a feeble nod. "Camila is right. We shouldn't have secrets between us after all these months. We love each other. And my love for you is genuine." I swallow hard. Tears sting my eyes, but I'm quick to blink them away. "You might want to sit down for this."

"I'm fine." He shakes his head. "I'm a homicide detective. I've seen it all, Bizzy. I promise, I'll be accepting of whatever it is you have to tell me."

"No." My voice wavers. "You haven't seen or heard this. I promise you that."

"Hey"—he pulls me close and dots a kiss to my forehead—"there is not one thing you can say to me that will have me rethinking my feelings for you." He pulls back and bears those pale gray eyes into mine. "You have my unconditional love. Just say it. That's the hard part. I've already accepted it."

My mouth opens and I take a quick breath. "Oh, Jasper." I press my forehead to his chest before meeting back up with those day-glow eyes. "What I'm about to tell you can impact our future. It's powerful enough to create a fissure in our relationship, leaving us with the before and after. You will never look at me the same after this. And— I'm sorry to say this, but Leo"—I shrug—"he knows. I didn't tell him. He stumbled upon it. And well, Camila sort of knows, too, but that's a little more complicated."

"What?" He inches back as if he were baffled already. "Bizzy, please, tell me what's going on. I can take it. I promise we will survive."

"I don't know"—my voice quivers—"I don't know if we will." I try to pull away, but he only increases his hold on me.

"Yes"—a dull laugh rumbles in his chest—"do not doubt this. We will survive. Take a deep breath and just say it."

Sherlock and Fish blink through my mind. A part of me thought I'd be saying this to Jasper in the safety of my cottage with my furry best friends right there to support me. But then, it's probably best they don't witness the carnage.

"Okay," I pant and suddenly passing out feels like a very real option. I look into Jasper's beautiful eyes. "Here's the truth." The words come out breathy, almost inaudible. "When I was a teenager, Mackenzie Woods pushed me into a whiskey barrel filled with water. I almost drowned, and I have never been the same ever since. After that, for reasons I can't explain, I was able to hear things other people weren't privy to. I could hear things that they weren't saying—not out loud. I could hear their private thoughts."

"What?" He ticks his head to the side. "Like it increased your intuition?" He looks at me sideways, and I can see him quickly trying to make sense of this.

"No." I shake my head. "I could hear directly into people's private thoughts. It's true. I can read minds. Not every mind but most minds—your mind." I give a little shrug as I quiver right down to my bones.

His eyes scan over my features. "Like some party trick? I pick a number and you try to guess?"

"I don't need to guess, Jasper. You could pick a thousand numbers and I'd get them all right."

Seventeen.

"Seventeen."

Four.

"Four."

Five hundred and twenty-three.

"Five hundred and twenty-three."

His grip loosens over my arms as he takes a staggering step back.

"I've been reading your mind since the moment we met. I don't mean to pry. It's just an open frequency to me. I'm sorry, Jasper. But I know your thoughts, your private musings. I know what you're thinking about and who. And there is no way for you to hide it. At least not when you're near me. I'm not very good at hearing things that aren't next to me. But you are almost always next to me. And I can't find the shut-off valve." I swallow hard. "Can you ever forgive me?"

His Adam's apple rises and falls as his eyes widen, but there's a vacancy there. Jasper isn't sure what to make of what I've just said to him, and not a single coherent thought has formulated.

How does this work? How are we going to work?

"I don't know how it works," I say, affirming his thoughts, and his eyes sharpen over mine. "And I don't know how we're going to work either."

I speed out of his office, out of the sheriff's department, jump back into my car, and drive all the way to Cider Cove.

Jasper doesn't call or text. He doesn't stop by in the evening. He doesn't pick up Sherlock that night. In fact, Jasper's truck never makes it back into his driveway.

For all I know he's left the country.

One thing I'm pretty certain about is the fact we're over for good.

Tomorrow is Valentine's Day and I need to put on a happy face for the guests at the inn and the guests at the community center.

And I don't know how I'm ever going to get through it all.

Fish, Sherlock, and Cinnamon all snuggle up with me in my bed, trying to assure me that he'll come around.

I don't know about that.

All I know is my love life is in shambles.

There is still a killer on the loose.

And since I can't do anything about the former, maybe I can do something about the latter.

18

Sherlock jumps in front of me as I examine myself in the full-length mirror nestled in my bedroom. I've donned a crimson dress that's cut down to there and sits up to here and has every racy curve highlighted for all to see.

Sherlock lets out a sharp bark. ***Jasper's eyes are about to fall out of his head when he sees you, Bizzy.***

"Sadly, I don't want to talk about Jasper," I say. It's Valentine's Day, or evening as it were. I barely ambled my way through the afternoon. It was harder than I thought keeping a cheery countenance for the guests.

Leo stopped by this morning, letting me know that Jasper called in sick, and so I told him what happened. He was as supportive as he could be. But he felt bad for me, too.

In less than an hour I'm set to deliver all those sweet treats the Country Cottage Café baked for the dance at the community center. And I've coerced nearly all my guests into going. I figured I should at least make an appearance before I come home to cry myself to sleep.

Fish hops onto my bed and bleats a simple meow. ***Do you think the killer will be there tonight, Bizzy?***

"Oh, I know she will. I called both Emily and Paige and extended the invite. And I assured them that the Dependable app had nothing to do with it. They both said they'd stop by."

That's another motivator for going. A part of me is anxious to pull a confession from either one of them.

Cinnamon skips on over and I pick up the curly cutie.

Bizzy, be careful. One of them killed Lad. She didn't hesitate to do it. Who knows what she'll do to you once she knows you learned the truth?

"She won't do anything." I dot her head with a kiss. "I can promise you that. I'll be coming home safe and sound."

And alone.

But I keep that bit of depressing news to myself.

The Cider Cove Community Center looks more or less like an overgrown school gym. And with all the pink and red balloons, the Valentine cutouts, and the jars of conversation hearts strewn all around, tonight it very much holds the appeal of a cheesy high school dance as well. The lights are dim, romantic music filters through the speakers, and couples are already moving on the dance floor. It's about as romantic as can be, and the entire Cupid-based scene makes me want to puke.

No sooner do Emmie and I finish setting out the raspberry cheesecake bites than she scuttles off to speak with a dark-haired deputy who just so happened to stroll in.

Good Lord, she's got no shame in her stealing-your-man game. She's liable to end up as the next body to turn up in Cider Cove if she keeps this up.

I spot Emily and Paige entering through the large heart-shaped arch made exclusively of Mylar balloons, and something in me quickens at the sight of them. I'm about to head that way when a body steps in front of me, and I look up to see a genuine fire in Mackenzie Woods' eyes.

A breath hitches in my throat.

"Mayor Woods," my voice squeaks. If there's anything I don't want tonight, it's to be caught up in a potentially deadly love triangle.

"What in Emmie Crosby's name is going on here?" she growls, and I take a moment to decide if Mack just invoked Emmie's name as a curse.

"I don't know what you're talking about," I say, trying to get around her.

She sucks in a quick breath and blocks my path once again. "You're in on this! Oh, Bizzy Baker, you will rue the day you decided to cover for that little pop tart you call a bestie. I can't believe she's the turnip that overturned my apple cart."

Good Lord, Mackenzie is mixing up her euphemisms, a very bad sign if you ask me. If her brain is misfiring, there's no telling what direction she'll launch her next missile.

"Look, Mack, I have no idea what's going on between the two of them. But wasn't it you who said you dumped him? If that's true, then he's a free agent—able to persue whomever he wishes, even Emmie Crosby. Now, if you'll excuse me..." I barrel past her without giving her a reason for my abrupt exit. But it's too late. I've lost Emily and Paige in this sea of people. Instead, I stumble upon a couple of happy-go-lucky kaftan wearing beauties swinging their hips to the rhythm of the music all by their lonesome.

"Bizzy Baker!" Georgie pulls me into their hip gyrating midst. "Now we've got a party. Where's that hotshot detective of yours? I know he hasn't seen you in that fitted red dress yet or he wouldn't have let you out of his sight."

She's right about the dress. It is aggressively curve hugging, and I was hoping if Jasper did see me, he would do just as she suggested.

"I don't know where he is." It's the horrible, horrible truth. "How about you two? Any men on the agenda tonight?" That didn't come out exactly how I meant it to, but I don't bother clearing it up either.

Juni lets out a whoop. "Spike will be here shortly. The beefy security guard from the Pawn King? We're sort of a thing. I'm thinking of moving in with him next week."

My mouth falls open, but I'm too jaded by my own impetuous love life to give her any advice on matters of the heart.

Georgie slaps her on the back. "That's my Juniper Moonbeam. Stealing hearts and finding a new roof to go over her head all at once." She tightens her smile as she looks my way. "And I've got Archer stopping by. He's the nude nudie we were lucky enough to meet at the art center. My mother always said when fate throws a naked man in your face, you had better heed that horny call. And I'm heeding it in about ten minutes." She elbows me in the ribs. "And I'll be out of here in twelve. We're heading back to my place for a little dessert. If the cottage is a rockin', don't come a knockin'."

"I won't," I'm quick to assure her. "Unless, of course, it's on fire. The two of you do share a rather inflammatory history, in the most literal sense."

They fall into a fit of laughter at the thought, and I migrate my way farther into the crowd in hopes to find at least one of the Carter women.

The last month runs through my mind.

That fated night blinks before me in flashes as I try my best to put together the pieces.

I'm pretty sure Colt Ferguson didn't pull the trigger. He was pretty unhappy that Lad wasn't around to pay back all the money he owed him. And then there's Madeline. She seemed to be content being the third woman in line to get Lad's attention. Lad was such a sleaze. But did he deserve a bullet? I mean, people can be rehabilitated from all sorts of addictions, gambling, even an addiction to women. And it certainly sounds as if Lad had his fair share of addictions.

Paige hated him for what he was doing to her mother. But would she really pull the trigger?

And not once did I pick up that Emily was covering for her daughter.

Funny. Not once did I pick up that Paige was covering for her mother.

Maybe whichever of them did kill Lad didn't tell the other? Maybe they wanted to keep it to themselves in order to keep the other person from turning into an accessory to the murder?

And then there's Natalie.

She was so in love with the guy she was willing to overlook the fact Lad was just using Emily to fund his gambling addiction. She went so far as agreeing to some ominous accident that was about to befall poor Emily. She had to trust him to keep his word. I mean, the guy was about to get married.

If Jasper were about to get married to Camila, I wouldn't be onboard, not for any amount of money, not even if we were going to arrange an accident to befall her someday. I mean, how could anyone in that situation trust a thing a guy like that would say?

What if he was a pathological liar in addition to being a gambler?

What if I suspected he were lying? What if I caught him in that lie?

I would kill him.

Mayor Woods runs up. "Bizzy Baker!" she growls my name out like a threat. "Emmie is climbing Leo as if he were Mount Granger. You know what that means?"

"No, actually." But I'm not paying much mind to Mack at the moment.

Natalie... Sure, I don't know what she was capable of. But humans are capable of just about anything when pushed to the limit.

Mackenzie growls as she glares into the crowd, "I'm going to kill her."

She takes off one way, and I take off the next.

A conversation I had with Natalie comes back to me. It was the night of Dependable's big do-over at the inn. She mentioned she should feel terrible about being there, but that it was nice to be out there again to meet someone— someone who actually knows what it means to keep their word.

Of course, that last part was an internal musing, but I caught it.

And now I'm wondering what I might have missed.

I spot Natalie lingering by the dessert table and I head her way.

Something tells me I'm about to fill in the deadly details.

19

"Bizzy!" Natalie toasts me with a raspberry cheesecake bite. "These are everything. They came from the café at the inn, right?"

"They did." It comes out lackluster.

Natalie Weiland has her hair teased up top to give it a little fullness, and her crimson lipstick and dress match the exact hue of her tresses.

She moans through a bite. "I'll stop by tomorrow and pick up a dozen or so for the bookshop. Everyone will just love them. Oh hey? Did you ever share that secret with your boyfriend?"

A heavy feeling comes over me, and suddenly I'd much rather be back at my cottage with my covers pulled over my head, snuggling with my pets.

"I did. It sort of backfired on me." I shrug. "I guess I know how he feels now."

"Oh no!" She pulls me into a quick embrace, and I can practically taste her sugary perfume. "I'm so sorry." She pulls back with genuine sorrow in her eyes.

"Believe me, I'm sorry, too. But I'm sort of not dealing with that right now. I mean, it's Valentine's Day. Practically all of the guests from the inn are here. I'll have to emotionally unpack it all later." Alone, weeping into my pillow. Just like last night.

"Don't you worry, Bizzy. If he's going to be petty, then he wasn't the one for you. Chin up, girl. There are plenty of eligible men here tonight."

I glance out at the crowd and spot my sister doing an odd little thumb jabbing dance in the middle of the crowd. I'm betting she spiked her own punch. *Have vodka flask will travel* seems to be her new motto.

Emily and Paige walk by chattering amongst themselves, and by some sheer miracle they didn't seem to notice us by the refreshment table.

"There she goes." Natalie rolls her eyes. "Can you believe it? Lad's not even cold in the grave and here Emily is, trolling for men."

"Their wedding was just weeks away." I nod. "I bet they had a fancy honeymoon planned. Probably somewhere exotic." And I think I know where.

She nods as she takes another quick bite. "Turks and Caicos." She shrugs. *I'm still going. No use in letting a perfectly good resort go to waste. Can you imagine if Emily went, too? Now that would be a hoot.*

Knew it.

"Turks and Caicos? You really were good friends with Lad, weren't you?"

She takes a deep breath. "Too good."

"I saw the paintings you did at Carter's corporate office."

Her eyes widen, and the red spotlights up above us wash over her, giving her a devilish appeal.

"Bizzy, what are you talking about?"

"The paintings. Emily showed them to me. They were painted by Land Wei. Lad bought them. You painted them, right? Land Wei—*Weiland*? I stopped by the bookshop to talk to you yesterday, and one of your coworkers mentioned you used the back as a studio. I took a look at one of the canvases. The painting was identical to the ones at the art center. And it was signed by you—Land Wei. You worked with Lad in an effort to help him bilk Emily out of her millions."

She shakes her head vehemently. "It wasn't millions." Her fingers rise to her lips as if she's realizing her blunder.

"I also took a look at that calendar sitting on the desk in the back of the bookstore. You have two weeks off in May. It says you'll be in T&C. That stands for Turks and Caicos, doesn't it?"

"I have to go." She takes a few wooden steps for the door, and I block her.

"You were having an ongoing affair with Lad Warner. The two of you planned to bilk Emily out of all her money, and then you were going to stage an accident. That's what the two of you argued about that night at the inn, isn't it?"

"You heard?" she pants as she gives a quick look around.

Natalie pushes past me, running through the kitchen, and I follow her straight into the parking lot in back of the community center where the air holds a dangerous chill.

"Don't follow me, Bizzy." She fishes her keys out of her purse and quickly looks around as if trying to orient herself. "I'm sorry. I have to go. You should forget all about any of that. I'm not a bad person."

"You killed him, didn't you? Lad had a garish pink lip print on his cheek that night. The same hue that Paige wears."

Her eyes catch to mine. *I'll go with it.* "Yes. Paige probably kissed him when she greeted him. Or right before she pulled the trigger."

"No." I shake my head. "I don't know why I didn't piece this together earlier. When I saw you after the murder, your lipstick was smudged. You had taken it off. Your mascara was running, too, because you were upset. You came there that night knowing you were going to kill Lad. You tried to frame Paige. And when that didn't work, you outright accused her and Emily. Although it was so probable, you didn't have to do a lot of convincing."

"They must have done it." She shakes her head. **Nobody knows I did it. And if I get my way, they never will.**

My breath blows out in a white plume.

"But if I get my way, Natalie, everyone will know."

Her eyes widen with terror. "How did you—?"

"You killed Lad because you didn't trust him. You were insecure."

She gives an incredulous groan. "How I hate that word. Don't say that to me!" She holds her hands over her ears. "I never want to hear that again. I loved him! There, I said it." Her voice roars, garbled with grief. "I loved him. He wanted me to wait for him. He promised me six months is all it would take, but then he said that he might need more time. I couldn't do it. I couldn't be the other woman forever. What about me? What about *my* life, Bizzy? Emily was going to win. She was going to have him."

"How did you get the gun? Did Lad give you the gun he bought for Emily?" And then it hits me like a ton of bricks. "Oh my God, the guy at the pawn shop said Lad was buying the gun for an artist friend of his. You were that friend." I shake my head as I look at her with the moon shining over her like a spotlight.

"I asked for it." Her voice trembles. "If Emily caught wind of our plan, there was no telling what she would do to me. She's a very powerful woman with powerful connections. I didn't want to be confronted then, just like I don't now." She pulls a gun out of her purse with a shaky hand, and soon enough I'm staring down a fidgeting barrel. "I left that gun where someone like you could find it. I didn't want anyone searching for it, searching for me. But I was wrong about that, wasn't I, Bizzy? The very next day I went back to the Pawn King and picked this one up for myself. Emily is still out there. But little did I know it was you I'd have to protect myself from. I'm sorry, Bizzy. One shot to the heart. It's not what anyone would want for Valentine's Day, but you asked for it. You put your nose where it didn't belong, and this is what you'll get in return."

The sound of hooves, or paws trampling this way, garners her attention, and as soon as she glances around, I lunge forward and latch onto the weapon.

Bizzy! A freckled beast flashes against the ground as an all too familiar dog bounds his way over.

"Sherlock?" I shout just as the gun goes off and the blast sends me flying.

Natalie lands face-first onto the ground before crawling away as fast as she can.

"Sherlock, stop her!" I scream, and Sherlock jumps onto her back as if he were hopping on for a ride. It takes me less than five seconds to do the same just as she tries to turn the gun on me once again.

In a moment she's on top of me, and Sherlock all but goes for the jugular.

"Freeze! Seaview Sheriff's Department!" Jasper's familiar voice booms over the vicinity, and everything in me seizes.

Leo appears from nowhere and tackles Natalie to the ground. And just like that, it's over.

Bizzy, are you okay? Sherlock says while licking my face as I struggle to rise.

"I'm okay," I whisper, unsure if it's true at all.

A strong pair of arms helps me to my feet, and suddenly I'm face to face with a pair of eyes that flash like lightning.

"Bizzy." Jasper pulls me into a hard embrace, peppering my face with kisses, before landing a single heated, lingering kiss over my lips. "I love you, Bizzy Baker. I don't care about anything else. I'm sorry. I had to pull myself together for a moment. But I'm not going anywhere.

I'm still here if you'll have me." He pulls back and bears his gaze into mine. *I love you, Bizzy Baker. Nothing else matters. I love every part of you. Even this one.*

A smile grows steadily over my face.

"I love you, too, Jasper." I'm about to seal it with another delicious kiss when Sherlock jumps up on us.

"Whoa," I say, giving him a hug as well. "You saved me. Thank you, Sherlock."

The parking lot quickly fills up with deputy vehicles flashing a steady stream of blue and red.

Sherlock barks. *Are you back together? Is everything better now?*

I nod up at Jasper. "Everything's better now." I shrug. "Turns out, I can read his mind, too."

His lips part before he gives a silent laugh. "Just when I didn't think you could surprise me any more than you already have." He bites down over his lip. "Speaking of surprises, I have one for you."

Sherlock gives a sharp bark.

"Okay, fine," Jasper says, looking down at his furry friend. "Sherlock Bones and I have a surprise for you."

"*Aww*," I coo as I give Jasper's rough stubble a quick scratch. "I can't wait to see it."

"Then let's go." Jasper pulls me in for another quick kiss.

And all is right with the world again.

The Country Cottage Inn glows with a pink aura as the evening expands into rich velvet darkness. The sky is glittering with stars and the moon bathes the cove and the evergreens that reach beyond its borders in silver.

Fish, Sherlock, and Cinnamon lead the charge, undeterred by the fact the woods are cloaked in darkness. But in the distance, near the bluff, there is an incandescent glow and my heart stops at the sight of it.

"Oh my God, Jasper, I think there's a fire." I pull out my phone in haste. "I need to call Jordy. What am I saying? I need to call the fire department."

Jasper gently lands his hand over mine, lowering the phone with the weight of his arm.

"There's no fire, I promise. No harm will come to the woods or the inn."

My mouth falls open. "What are you up to?"

Jasper pulls me close as we follow the trail that leads to the cliff side, and as soon as we crest the bend in the forest, I see it.

"Jasper Wilder." I take a breath and hold it. "What in the world?"

The gazebo is softly illuminated by dozens of paper bags with hearts punched out in the center of them, and they shimmer into the night as they flicker with a peachy glow.

Electric candles. Jasper brushes a kiss into my hair. *Jordy helped me set them up. He was afraid I might have burned down all of Maine.*

A bubbling laugh comes from me. "That sounds like Jordy." And like me.

Fish lets out a sharp meow. *Bizzy Baker! This is magical. Jasper has quite a way of saying I'm sorry. I think the two of you should fight more often.*

"Fish says this place is magical. She's also not opposed to us fighting."

Fish growls. *Only if the end result is this beautiful. For goodness' sake, tell him, Bizzy. He's going to think I'm a furry little monster.*

I quickly relay it to Jasper and he chuckles.

He gives her a quick pat. "You're the best cat I know, Fish. I could never think less of you. We're family."

Sherlock lets out a few good barks. *They did not fight, Fish. Jasper just needed a moment to think.*

"Sherlock insists we didn't fight," I say. "He says you just needed a moment to think."

"And that's the truth." He winces my way. "But rest assured, I will never do that again."

"Rest assured, I won't throw any more telepathic surprises at you."

Cinnamon runs over and lets out a few happy little yips. *I found the treats! I found the treats!* She takes off back into the gazebo, and soon the three of them are snarling and wrestling for biscuits and—

"Is that bacon?" I ask as we're about to crest the gazebo.

"That would be bacon. I figured I owed everyone an apology."

"You don't owe me anything," I say as I take in the oversized gazebo glowing like the inside of a jack-o-lantern, sending its flickering incandescence into the sky like a love song. The wrought iron roses are lit up a pale pink and it looks enchanting, straight from a fairytale where happy endings abound.

Jasper leads me inside and we pause as we stand in the middle of all the magical splendor. His eyes sparkle like cut diamonds as he bears his gaze to mine.

"Bizzy Baker, I have a confession to make." He gives our hands a gentle swing. "I have been mesmerized by you since the moment I first laid eyes on you."

I bite down over my lower lip in an effort to keep my emotions in check.

His chest expands unreasonably wide with his next breath.

"I have never met a person quite like you, as kind, as strong, as capable, as determined—even when we're not in complete agreement. But your heart for justice appeals to mine in so many ways. Your ability to winnow out a killer has confounded me. You have left me baffled. You challenge me. You make me a better person by simply being near me. That day I stumbled upon the inn, I thought this might be a good place to settle until I found something new. And because of you, I never want to leave. I'd like to believe it was fate that led me to you that day and destiny that leads us to this one. Regardless, it has only been good fortune having you as a part of my life." He swallows hard, his features grow far too serious, and for a brief moment I'm afraid this conversation might take a dark turn. "Some say life is a journey for one. I don't think it should be that way. I say this is a journey for two."

His silver eyes penetrate mine. His thoughts are fully encapsulated with love, and yet it's as if he's shielding me from them.

Jasper drops to one knee, and my heart gives an unnatural thump at the sight.

Fish, Sherlock, and Cinnamon start in on a choir of yowls and howls. Their excitement only highlights my own.

"Bizzy Baker"—Jasper trains his eyes on mine—"they say when you meet the right one, you just know. And if I know anything at all, it's that you're the right one for me. I don't need another decade to affirm this. This is a truth that is unchanging for me, and I hope it is for you. I want to spend the rest of my life with you, Bizzy. I want to share every adventure this world can bring. I want to have children with you. Together, we can build a family. You are my family. Bizzy Baker, will you do me the honor of becoming my Valentine for the rest of my days? Will you do me the honor and become my wife?"

Jasper holds up the ring. Its brilliance catches the moonlight and shoots it off in all directions like a prism.

"*Yes!*" I don't hesitate with the answer, and just like that, my body bucks and every emotion I've been holding back bursts to the forefront in the form of laughter and tears.

Jasper glides the ring over my finger before he stands and spins me in a dizzying circle.

We seal our affection with a kiss, to the sound of the waves, the sound of three incredibly happy pets, and the rhythmic thundering of our hearts.

20

Valentine's Day has always been a cheerful occasion, a bright spot in an otherwise dreary month. But for the rest of my life, this day will mark something momentous for me: the start of my family with Jasper.

News like this is too good to keep to ourselves, so we tuck Fish, Sherlock, and Cinnamon to bed at my cottage and head back to the community center.

The crowd is thick inside as soft melodic music filters from the speakers, inspiring couples to migrate toward the dance floor.

We spot Georgie, Juni, my father, mother, and Jasper's mother talking by the dessert table.

Macy is still bopping in a circle, dancing to the beat of her own drummer, literally, and I snatch her as we make our way to the back.

"Hey!" She bumps my hip with hers. "I was having fun."

"How about a quick cheesecake break?"

She moans at the thought. "Good idea." She waves to Jasper. "I'll take another sweetheart punch. Make it a double!"

It's clear Macy has had her fair share of doubles tonight.

I spot Emmie and Mackenzie by the refreshment table and veer left as I link arms with my bestie.

"Excuse us, Mayor Woods."

Emmie leans in. "Nice save. Did you know it was bad form for the mayor to get in a knock-down, drag-out fight?"

"Lucky you."

"Yeah, but she said she'd meet up with me in a dark alley. She also suggested I sleep with one eye open."

"That's only because she's ticked that she'll be sleeping alone. Apparently, she dumped Leo before the two of you locked lips. Are you really serious about the guy?"

"I don't know. He's hot. I'm all for seeing where it goes. We're just having a good time."

Emmie has had a long list of men she's had a good time with. I'm hoping she'll settle soon. Which brings me to my next point.

Jasper pulls me close as we stand in a circle of our loved ones, and as soon as we've gathered their attention, I hold out my left hand.

"I said yes!"

The small crowd breaks out into a cheer as congratulations erupt from everyone around us. My mother is the first to pull me in tight.

"Bizzy!" She leans in and whispers, "Make sure to keep your name. Oh, what the heck, you can hyphenate if you want to." She pulls back, her eyes sparkling with tears. "I'm so very happy for you. I can't wait to experience it all, the dress, the wedding, the glorious reception."

Georgie topples over me with a firm embrace. "When's the big day?"

Macy yanks her to the side. "Are you knocked up?"

"No." I wave my sauced-up sister away.

Juniper Moonbeam makes a face. "Don't waste any time. He's a walking specimen. There will be twelve different women after him until the day he bites the big one."

Emmie shoves her off before I can figure out a response.

"You don't have to do anything you don't want to." She offers me a hearty embrace. "You have so many options. And I want to be a part of it all. I'll be right there by your side, supporting whatever you choose."

Dad comes in and warms me with his strong arms as he encapsulates me with a hug.

"Bizzy Bizzy." He pulls back with tears glinting in his eyes. "You're going to make a grown man cry. You'll be a beautiful bride. Can't wait, kiddo."

He's quick to pull Jasper into a warm embrace, too. "Be good to her. She's solid gold."

"I will, Nathan." Jasper nods. "And I agree. She's invaluable."

Gwyneth steps forward. Her dark hair is neatly pulled back and her dark gown sparkles in the dim light.

She examines me a moment. "What the heck"—she says as she tosses her hands in the air—"welcome to the family." *She'll make a fine starter wife. I just hope Nathan and I survive the fallout.*

A breath gets locked in my throat as I pull away, but the music has shifted again to something a little more upbeat and Georgie and Juni are whooping it up.

Macy pulls my left hand toward her as Emmie huddles in.

My sister lifts a brow. "Emerald cut, encrusted with smaller diamonds that drip over the band on either side. Nice choice, Detective." She gives my hand a quick wiggle. "My guess is two point five carats. I guess he's a keeper."

A laugh gets caught in my throat as I look to Jasper.

He nods to my sister. "I'm glad you approve, Macy." Jasper shifts his attention my way. "And just for the record, I talked to both your dad and your brother beforehand and asked for their permission."

"You did?" My heart melts just hearing it.

He nods. "Hux sends his congratulations. That is, if you said yes. And he wanted me to tell you right out the gate, he's drawing up a prenup."

"That sounds like my brother." I mouth a quick *sorry*.

His cheek rises on one side and there's a glazed look taking over his eyes that I wholeheartedly approve of.

Just as I'm about to wrap my arms around him, Leo Granger pops up.

He nods to the both of us. "I hear congratulations are in order."

Jasper stiffens a moment. **Here we go.**

"Thank you, Leo," I say and Jasper does the same with a lot less enthusiasm. I know Jasper is still wary of his old best friend, and I don't want him to be.

I take up Jasper's hand and ask Leo to follow us a few feet away from the crowd.

"Leo, I told Jasper something very private about myself. But you already know that. I think maybe we should all talk about it." **And anything else you want to add, Leo.**

Jasper inches back as he widens his eyes my way. ***That's right. You mentioned Leo and Camila knew.*** A sigh expels from him as he looks back to the man he once regarded as a brother.

"Bizzy said you figured it out," Jasper starts out curt. "How'd you do it?"

Leo exhales as he glances my way.

"What do you think?" Leo shrugs and I nod over to him. "Fine." He closes his eyes a moment. "I'm sorry, Jasper. I wanted to tell you sooner. But—I'm actually just like Bizzy. That's what led me to her. And that's the only thing that has ever been between us." He lifts his hands as if it were a stickup. Leo swallows hard. "It's not just us. My aunt can do it, too."

Jasper's features elongate as he sobers up on a dime.

Leo continues. "I'm not sure if Bizzy told you, but this gift—it's something called transmundane. Our quirk is further classified as telesensual. Camila picked up on the fact I could read her mind while we were seeing each other. I confessed. I thought it'd bring us closer. I was wrong. I'm glad things turned out differently for the two of you." He holds out his hand and Jasper shakes it before pulling Leo into a partial embrace. "Congratulations. I couldn't have picked a better woman for you, man."

"Thank you." Jasper's eyes are still set wide as he struggles to digest this new information. "This is going to take a minute to set in."

"Take all the time you need, buddy." Leo slaps him on the back before pulling me into a hug as well. "I'll see you both around."

We watch as he heads over to Emmie and the two of them are quickly swept into the sea of bodies moving to the music.

Soon, I'm in Jasper's arms and we're doing the exact same thing.

"This is a perfect ending to a perfect night." He presses a kiss to my temple.

I pull back and bite down over my lip. "Perfect indeed. But we can always improve upon perfection. Dessert at my place?"

Jasper's lids hood low with naughty intent and a devilish smile twitches at his lips.

"Now that sounds perfect."

Jasper and I indulge in a molten hot kiss that's a preview of the sizzling future.

It's going to be a good one.

I can feel it deep down in my bones.

In the morning, despite the magical fireworks last night produced, I'm right back at the reception counter with Grady and Nessa, checking out old guests and welcoming in the new.

Fish and Sherlock are in a prime mood, super excited they're officially family now. And Cinnamon is in a stellar mood herself, because she just so happens to be in her new mama's arms.

Emmie drops a kiss to the cutie's little red head.

"I'm so in love with her," she coos. "And her name is perfect." She kisses the pup's furry forehead once again. "And guess who can't wait to walk her?"

"Jordy?" I have a feeling her brother was not the right answer, but I don't dare take a stab at the right one.

"Stop," she teases. "It's Leo. How about we do a double date? Pizza and a movie? It'll be like high school all over again."

"Yeah, but with better boyfriends." I wiggle my left hand her way. "I'd add that Mackenzie won't be there to steal them, but I'm not too sure about that. You do realize you've got a target on your back."

Emmie's lips twitch. "I know. And from what Leo tells me, you've got one, too. Camila is a genuine stalker."

"Hey? Maybe we can take out a double restraining order on Camila and Mack?"

Someone clears their throat from behind and we turn to find Mackenzie herself looking as if someone peed on her cheesecake bites.

"Mayor Woods," I say, bellying up to the reception counter. "How can I help you today?"

She glares over at Emmie and me. "Just wanted to let you know there's a baking competition for senior citizens set for the middle of May. The community center is out. It's booked for a dental convention. I thought I'd see if the inn would be looking to host. The portable ovens will be on loan from the culinary school in Seaview, but it's Cider Cove's turn to host the event, and I don't want to lose out on all the revenue it can generate just because we're crawling up the wazoo with a bunch of ridiculous dentists."

Emmie bites down on her lip. "Don't disparage the dentists, Mack. There might just be a hot one in the bunch."

Mackenzie belts out a genuine growl.

"Yes," I say. "The middle of May is perfect."

"Good." Mackenzie spits it out like an expletive. Leave it to Mack to turn a four-letter word into a *four-letter word*. "We'll need a panel of ten judges. And I'll need you to help elect them."

"Me?" I point to my chest.

"Yes, you. This is an amateur event. We want local bakers, but one or two should be from somewhere else in New England. The city will comp their weekend stay at the inn. I'll see you later." She turns to Emmie, and I can't help but note a current of danger in the air. "You'll regret the day you looked at Leo Granger." And with that, she takes off.

"Bakers," I say as I hit the internet hard. "Pick a state in New England, Emmie."

"Vermont. That would be a nice place to ship Mack off to, don't you think?"

"Only if you don't mind all of Vermont hating us."

I quickly type in *bakeries in Vermont.*

"Ha," I say. "Look at this. The very first one that pops up is an adorable place called the Cutie Pie Bakery and Cakery. It says, *baker Lottie Lemon takes the cake.* I think we found our first guest judge. That is, if she agrees to do it. And if she does, that's one baker down."

A large bouquet of at least two-dozen long-stem roses heads this way, cleverly hiding the identity of their owner. The flowers drop a notch, revealing a pair of stunning silver eyes.

Jasper hands me the bouquet and both Emmie and I swoon.

His lips curve my way. "Rumor has it that my fiancée runs this place."

"With an iron fist," I tease as I skip around the counter and attack him with my lips.

"You own my heart, Bizzy. How about we head to the café and have breakfast? I hear we have a wedding to plan."

"We've got a wedding to plan!" I squeal at the thought as we head off for the café with Fish and Sherlock hot on our tails.

It feels as if I'm walking on air, on a Valentine.

Valentine's Day may have come and gone, but I have a feeling the effect of Cupid's arrow will live on forever in Jasper and me.

I know it will.

We have forever.

And soon, we'll say I do.

Recipe

Country Cottage Café
Raspberry Cheesecake Bites

Hello there! It's me, Bizzy Baker! The Country Cottage Café has out done themselves this time. If you're a fan of cheesecake, you are going to fall in love with this recipe. Emmie can't stop making them, and I can't stop eating them. They're a favorite of Jasper's too. This one is a keeper!

Ingredients

Crust
1 ½ cup graham cracker crumbs
7 tablespoons butter

Cheesecake
8 oz. white chocolate chips
¼ cup half and half
1 package cream cheese (8 ounces) softened
¼ cup sugar
2 large eggs

1 teaspoon vanilla extract

1   12 oz. package of raspberries (fresh is best)

Instructions

Preheat oven to 325°

Crust
Mix graham cracker crumbs and butter until well blended. Place in bottom of miniature cupcake cups, pressing down until crust is formed.

Cheesecake
Add white chocolate chips and half and half in a saucepan until white chocolate chips are melted. In a separate mixing bowl combine softened cream cheese and sugar. Mix well until smooth. Beat eggs, then add slowly. Stir in vanilla. Add white chocolate chip mixture (once cooled). Place mixture into cupcake cups, dispersing evenly.

Bake for 20 minutes. Let cool to room temperature then cover and set in the refrigerator overnight. Once chilled, top with fresh raspberries.

Enjoy! These will go fast!

Acknowledgements

Thank you so much for coming along on this fun adventure with us! We hope you love Cider Cove and all of its crazy residents as much as we do. We're so jazzed to share the next book with you, Felines and Fatalities (Country Cottage Mysteries 6)! It's a crossover with Murder in the Mix Mysteries and a murderously good time will be had by all. If you're a fan of Honey Hollow, you will not want to miss out on this one. Thank you so much from the bottom of our hearts for taking this roller coaster ride with us. We cannot wait to take you back to Cider Cove!

Special thank you to the following people for taking care of this book—Kaila Eileen Turingan-Ramos, Kathryn Jacoby, Jodie Tarleton, Ashley Daniels and Lisa Markson. And a very big shout out to Lou Harper of Cover Affairs for designing the world's best covers.

A heartfelt thank you to Paige Maroney Smith for being so amazing in every single way.

And last, but never least, thank you to Him who sits on the throne. Worthy is the Lamb! Glory and honor and power are yours. We owe you everything.

About the Author

Bellamy Bloom

Bellamy Bloom is a **USA TODAY** bestselling author who writes cozy mysteries filled with humor, intrigue and a touch of the supernatural. When she's not writing up a murderous storm she's snuggled by the fire with her two precious pooches, chewing down her to-be-read pile and drinking copious amounts of coffee.

Visit her at:

www.authorbellamybloom.com

Addison Moore

Addison Moore is a **New York Times, USA Today,** and **Wall Street Journal** bestselling author who writes mystery, psychological thrillers and romance. Her work has been featured in ***Cosmopolitan*** Magazine. Previously she worked as a therapist on a locked psychiatric unit for nearly a decade. She resides on the West Coast with her husband, four wonderful children, and two dogs where eats too much chocolate and stays up way too late. When she's not writing, she's reading. Addison's Celestra Series has been optioned for film by **20th Century Fox.**

Feel free to visit her at:

www.addisonmoore.com

Made in United States
Orlando, FL
01 April 2023

31623367R00161